~ Look for these titles from Max Rose ~

Now Available

The Omega's Heir
To Love an Omega
Reclaiming His Omega
Omega Rescue

OMEGA RESCUE

MM Mpreg Romance

Max Rose

etopia press

Etopia Press
1643 Warwick Ave., #124
Warwick, RI 02889
http://www.etopia-press.net

This book is a work of fiction. The names, characters, places, and incidents are fictitious or have been used fictitiously, and are not to be construed as real in any way. Any resemblance to persons, living or dead, actual events, locales, or organizations is entirely coincidental.

OMEGA RESCUE

Copyright © 2019 by Max Rose

All Rights Are Reserved. No part of this book may be used or reproduced in any manner whatsoever without written permission, except in the case of brief quotations embodied in critical articles and reviews.

First Etopia Press electronic publication: January 2019

First Etopia Press print publication: January 2019

~ DEDICATION ~

To Shelly for all her help.

CHAPTER ONE

Firefighter Darren Drake used his ax to smash his way into the top apartment of the burning three-story building. Breaking the door open was easy. His werewolf strength and the adrenaline racing through his veins gave him more than enough power with each blow.

His breath rasped loudly inside his self-contained breathing apparatus—the mask, oxygen tank, and harness he carried whenever he entered a burning building. The stink of smoke hung over everything, drowning out nearly every other scent. As a werewolf, he could smell the fire, even through the mask.

Darren didn't feel any fear. Instead, he only felt a sharp sense of urgency. He was searching the building for anyone trapped inside.

Without hesitation, he charged into the apartment, barely able to see with all the black-gray smoke swirling through the building.

Outside, 22nd Battalion Engine Company 80 was pouring water on the fire, drenching the roof. Water was raining down inside in places, but the fire was still going strong on the east side of the building where they were. Darren and Mack were part of a team checking for trapped victims. They had cleared the bottom two apartments and found no one.

He pushed past the foyer and deeper into the apartment. His friend Mack moved in behind him. As soon as Darren had stepped inside, he had the unshakable feeling someone was in the burning apartment.

He rushed forward into the smoke, focused on only one thing. Saving a person's life.

It didn't take long to find him.

A man was sprawled on the carpet of the living room. He was lying motionless on his stomach.

Another jolt of adrenaline hit Darren as he ran to the man's side. He didn't appear burned, but most fire deaths were from smoke inhalation.

He turned the man over to check for vital signs. When he saw the man's face, his world shook and time came to a standstill. His glance seemed to go on forever as time stretched. Primal instincts and wolf instincts hit him like a runaway train.

It didn't matter that he didn't have time for this nonsense right now. He couldn't look away.

The fallen man was handsome. He had tousled blonde hair. His features were fine and aristocratic, with full lips that looked more than perfect for kissing. A day's growth of blond stubble dusted his cheeks. He was lean and fit, dressed in a T-shirt and jeans.

The man was also a werewolf. Darren's own wolf immediately recognized that fact by the man's scent and aura. He wasn't a powerful wolf. Not an alpha like Darren was but an omega wolf. That realization immediately brought out all of Darren's fierce protective instincts. The sight of the omega lying unconscious on the floor hit Darren like a punch in the guts. The need to save this omega roared up from deep within him. It was primal. It was undeniable.

This wolf was his mate.

There was no denying the raw power of a wolf finding his true mate. It drove out every other thought. It gave him strength beyond even that of a werewolf.

Darren felt like he could rip open a hole in the wall with his bare hands and carry his mate to safety, leaping from three stories up without a worry.

He tried to reel himself in. He had to focus on his job, not the fact that this omega wolf was his mate. His job was getting this man—his mate—to safety. *Now*.

Quickly, he checked the man for injuries. He saw no burns. Like he'd suspected, that meant smoke inhalation was the threat.

He had to get the man out of here right away. He radioed to the team that he'd found a victim and was bringing him out. They would have EMTs ready to race the victim to the hospital.

Darren carefully lifted his mate onto his shoulder in a classic fireman's carry and turned toward the door. The only thing he could think of was getting his omega to medical attention. The thought was like an alarm bell sounding over and over in his head. As a werewolf, the man would be tough and resilient, but clearly he had been overcome by the smoke and needed Darren's help.

Mack had checked the rest of the apartment and radioed that it was clear. Then Mack stayed beside him as they quickly made their way down the stairs with the victim.

The smoke wasn't as bad in the building's lower floors. Darren burst out of the front of the apartment complex and was immediately hit with water spray as his fellow firefighters doused him with a wider, less-powerful stream.

He rushed his mate to the EMTs. They were waiting, alerted by his status call to the team.

The protective side of his wolf flared up again with surprising ferocity, not wanting to hand his mate over to strangers. That was absurd, as his mate *was* a stranger and he needed their help. He controlled the wolf with a mental snarl and helped put the man on the ambulance stretcher. The EMTs immediately loaded the man into the back of the ambulance.

Darren pulled off his breathing device and started to climb in after his mate. He didn't hesitate even though he was still wearing all the rest of his protective gear.

One of the EMTs moved to stop him from getting in.

"I'm riding with him," he growled at the EMT.

"No you're not," the EMT shot back. "Not with all that gear. And not without your captain's say-so."

Darren felt another snarl building inside him. How dare they try to keep him from his omega? Nothing would stop him from making sure his mate was safe. Nothing.

Before Darren could take out his pent-up worry and frustration on the EMT who was only doing his job,

Mack put a restraining hand on his shoulder.

"After we're done here, you can go visit him," Mack said. "He's going to be okay. You saved him. We still have a job to finish."

It was one thing to hear those words and another to know they were true. Right now, every part of him wanted to know they were true with one hundred percent certainty. He wanted to be sure the omega wolf—his mate—would be all right.

But his friend was right. He also had a job to do. The fire wasn't out. His fellow firefighters were counting on him.

He nodded and turned back to the fire. Hose teams were still pouring water on the building. The captain was barking orders. Across the street from the burning apartment, there were news vans and crowds of people watching the fire.

Darren put on his breathing device again, ready to head back into the fray. He had a job to do, but as soon as it was physically possible, he would be heading to the hospital emergency room to check on the omega wolf he'd saved. Nothing would stop him.

Well, *one* thing might.

Because he didn't even know the man's name.

CHAPTER TWO

Alex Carson woke up in a hospital bed. The overhead lights were so bright he had to squint. His head was pounding as if his brain was a steel drum someone was hitting with a sledgehammer. He groaned and stirred, trying to remember what had happened.

He'd been in the furnished apartment he'd been renting for the month. He'd been working on his laptop, reviewing photos he'd taken in a Brazilian rainforest in months ago that he hadn't had the time to properly sort. He had hundreds of digital photos to review, and that didn't even count the photos he'd taken on standard film. He'd been to Brazil on assignment, but he'd taken a few extra days on his own dime to photograph more of the country. He'd been hoping for some great shots to send to another nature magazine or to use the photos to score another assignment. But then what had happened?

His memories were still hazy. He frowned, trying to concentrate. His pounding headache didn't help. Maybe if he thought back further, it would come to him.

Alex had been in Chicago for a month for an art and photography show. They were featuring an entire wall of his work. He'd even sold half his pieces. But now the show was winding down. He was already looking for a new assignment to satisfy his footloose ways.

He rubbed his temple, blinking in the harsh hospital light. So he had been engrossed in looking at digital photos in the apartment's single bedroom…and then he'd noticed it was hot and hard to breathe. When he glanced up, there had been smoke curling along the ceiling. He remembered how surprised and terrified he'd been.

When he'd opened the bedroom door to escape, the rest of the apartment had been filled with smoke. He'd dropped to his hands and knees to crawl…but then he'd started coughing. He remembered how weak he'd felt and remembered the blackness creeping in at the edge of his vision. He'd quickly become disoriented. Panic had gripped him.

He must not have made it out on his own. Clearly, someone had saved him.

A warm hum of gratitude began inside him. Someone had carried him out when he couldn't make it. Someone had saved his life. Gritting his teeth against a throb of pain, he lifted his head to take in more of his surroundings.

He was in a hospital bed of course. An IV was in his arm, and a nose tube was feeding him oxygen.

As he peered around the hospital room, a nurse hustled in.

"Thank God, you're okay," she said, moving to take his pulse, then to check over the readouts on several beeping machines. "How are you feeling?"

"Like I fell out of a plane and got hit by a bus on the way down."

She nodded grimly. "You had a very close call. You're suffering from smoke inhalation. You're healing quickly because of your werewolf blood, but you need to take it easy and let your body repair itself."

"You don't have to tell me twice," he replied, leaning back and closing his eyes. Taking it easy sounded like heaven. He wasn't sure he could do anything else right now anyway. "Who saved me?"

"I'm sorry?"

He squinted at her. The lights in here really were too bright for his headache. "I asked who saved me."

"Oh, a firefighter, I'm sure," she said. She smiled at him. She was actually quite pretty, although he only went for other men, so flirting with her was a waste of both their time. Her smile was kind, though, and kindness was something he appreciated right now.

Especially since he'd just lost everything. Thousands of dollars' worth of cameras and gear. His laptop. All his clothes. He lived on the go as a photographer, traveling around the country and around the world, but what little he did have was vital to his existence.

As grateful as he was to be alive, he couldn't help but grieve over his lost camera and his likely burned-to-a-crisp hard drive with all the photos. Photos he'd needed to upload to get paid for but hadn't before the fire hit. He had online backup…but he had put off uploading the Brazil photos. He had no excuse for it either, and now he was going to pay the price.

What a disaster.

Before he could say anything else, a doctor arrived along with another nurse. The doctor told him he had some minor swelling of his mucous membranes and some respiratory distress. But his airway, breathing, and circulation were good now. He wanted to take X-rays and do some blood tests.

"You were a lucky man," the doctor said.

"I heard a firefighter saved my life."

"It's true," the doctor confirmed as he examined Alex's charts. "They are braver than I am, rushing into burning buildings. So you owe your guardian angel firefighter your thanks."

Alex nodded. "What was his name? The man who saved me?"

He owed the man his thanks *and* a bottle of the finest scotch. That was if he could afford scotch anymore after losing everything in the fire…

The doctor shrugged. "Don't know. Tell you what, if I find out, I'll let you know."

"Thanks, I appreciate it. If he shows up to see how I am, please send him in. I want to thank him in person."

The doctors and nurses finally left him alone. He could hear the busy hospital wing through the room's open door—doctors being paged, people talking, squeaking shoes on the tiles.

He closed his eyes, hoping to fall asleep again and give the pain medicine time to take care of his headache and his raw throat. The only other thing he could do while trapped in this bed was stay awake and worry about the future.

No, he wasn't going to worry. Things would turn out all right. Weren't wolves like cats, always landing on their feet? Maybe not, but Alex was determined to land on his feet. He might be an omega wolf without the ferocity, dominance, and raw strength of an alpha, but he had inner strength. That would see him through.

It had to.

Sometime later, there was a soft knock at his door. He hadn't been sleeping. He'd been lying there with his eyes closed, remembering the incredible beauty of the rainforest, the flowers and vines and lush vegetation. He opened his eyes and looked right into the gaze of the most stunning man he'd ever seen.

First of all, the man was big. Six-foot-two or three easy. He had short, dark hair and was clean shaven. He had a jaw that looked like it could break rocks. And those eyes, a hazel that by itself wasn't anything special, but the intensity behind those eyes certainly was.

The man was looking at Alex as if he were an oasis in the desert, a rabbit in front of a hungry wolf…the last ice cube in the tray and the water in his glass was warm. He snorted at that last silly thought, but his brain seemed to have careened out of control just at the sight of this guy.

The man wore jeans, boots, and a T-shirt. That T-shirt was molded to the man's broad chest and impressive, broad shoulders. He looked like he could bench press cars without breaking a sweat. He wasn't handsome the way male models were handsome, but there was a rugged, raw power to him that had Alex's inner wolf howling.

And when the man's scent reached him, his omega wolf really went wild. The man smelled like smoke and water and bravery, of sweat and forest and determination. He smelled like…he smelled like Alex's mate.

No. That was crazy. Alex was clearly still addled from the smoke. He'd been all over the world and had never found a mate. If anyone had asked, he would've said he didn't believe in true mates. It was a ridiculously romantic idea. It was an idea he liked, one he wished were true, but also something he didn't believe in.

"*Mate,*" his wolf said with undeniable finality. "*He is our mate.*"

"*Shut up and go to sleep,*" he told his wolf. "*You don't know what you're talking about.*"

"*Our mate,*" the wolf insisted.

He rolled his eyes. There was no use talking to a stubborn wolf. Especially when it came to other wolves.

Instead of arguing, he turned his focus back on his big, handsome guest.

He raised an eyebrow. "Are you sure you have the

right room?"

Please have the right room. Please have the right room.

"Are you Alex Mason?" the man asked, his deep voice seeming to rumble like thunder.

Again, Alex's inner wolf responded, throwing back its head and howling with joy. At the same time, a wave of desire went right through Alex, gathering in his groin. The wolf was convinced that they'd finally found their mate. But the human part of him was feeling horny right now, looking at this man who might or might not be his mate but was still sexy as hell.

"I am Alex Carson," he managed to reply. "Come in, please."

The man nodded and stepped inside. He walked across the room and took a seat near Alex. The expression on his face was intense but also concerned.

"I'm glad to see you're awake," the man said. "The doctors wouldn't tell me anything. But since you told them I could come visit you, they let me in." He met and held Alex's eyes. "Thank you for inviting me to come see you."

It was a strangely formal thing to say, but being thanked by this man sent a thrill racing through Alex's body from his brain down to his cock.

Whoa there, boy, he thought as he shifted in the bed a little. He wasn't in good enough health to be this riled up. He was supposed to be taking it easy.

Besides that, he didn't want the unpredictable part of him that dangled between his legs to embarrass them both by standing up and leaving a clear-as-day tent in the sheets.

"So you're the firefighter who saved me," he said with a catch in his voice. "What's your name?"

"Darren Drake," the man replied roughly. Then he grinned. The grin gave him an almost boyish air.

Oh hell, this man was trouble. He was a werewolf, that was problem one.

Second, he was clearly an alpha. Even if he didn't have a pack of his own, he had the unmistakably powerful aura of an alpha.

And three, Alex's wolf kept insisting this Darren Drake was their mate.

Alex didn't need a calculator to know those three things added up to big trouble.

He managed to hide all the emotions and urges rioting inside him. Instead, he forced a smile onto his face to hide his nerves. "Thank you for saving my life, Mr. Drake."

The man shrugged. "My friends call me Darren."

Another thrill shot through Alex because it was clear Darren was giving him the opportunity to call him by his first name like a friend. He was being given the first name privilege with this alpha and they'd only known each other for minutes. It was crazy. His thoughts were reeling.

Maybe he was dreaming. Maybe he was in a coma right now, and this was his brain playing a cruel trick.

But if Darren was a trick, then Alex didn't want to ever wake up. His wolf snorted its agreement.

"I came to check on you," Darren continued. He seemed to be struggling not to say something he wanted to say. It was odd to see such a big, powerful wolf hesitate about anything. "Smoke inhalation can kill. I was worried. They rushed you off to the hospital before I knew for sure that you were okay. How is your throat? Does it hurt to talk?"

Alex shrugged. "It's a little uncomfortable, but they have me on meds. I should be fine. I'm a werewolf. I heal quick."

He admitted he was a wolf because he wanted to see if Darren would do the same. Of course, Darren could scent out that Alex was a wolf too, but Alex still wanted everything out in the open. There was a kind of formality to meeting another wolf. Especially an alpha.

Besides, he didn't like secrets. Never had. Sometimes he'd been accused of oversharing. Alex might bounce around the world as a freelance photographer, but that always remained the same.

Darren nodded solemnly. "I'm a werewolf too." His eyes narrowed. "You're an omega wolf."

Alex raised his chin defiantly. *Here we go again.* He was disappointed. It was always the same with these tough-guy wolves. Alphas were the worst.

"Not everyone can be an alpha, you know. So yes, I am an omega. But I'm no pushover."

The other man grinned. "Fair enough. I respect that."

They sat in silence for a little while. Alex was trying to come up with the right thing to say as his inner wolf kept whining or howling that they needed to be with their mate forever. The feelings were powerful. If he lost control of his thoughts for more than a second, his mind immediately filled with hot pictures of Darren from his out-of-control imagination. Images of Darren pinning him to the bed and capturing his lips in a fierce kiss. Or Darren lying back on a huge bed, sprawled naked and powerful, all muscles and brawn, and between his thick thighs a rock-hard cock jutting upward. A cock begging for Alex's lips around it—

No. Nope. Wild fantasies were taking over his brain. If he wasn't careful, he really was going to pitch a tent here in the sheets. And how would he explain that? As a side effect of smoke inhalation? No one would ever believe that.

"I'm an alpha," Darren said, shaking Alex out of his distracted thoughts. "I don't have a pack yet here in Chicago." Something about the man's tone said he was going to make this change and soon. Then he abruptly changed subjects. "I know you probably lost everything in the fire."

All Alex's friskiness immediately drained away at the mention of what he'd lost. All the stuff he needed to make a living as a photographer had been in that furnished flat he'd been renting.

He truly was in trouble. Panic began to flutter in his mind again.

"I did," he finally admitted. "Was everyone else in the building okay?"

Darren nodded. "No one else was home at the time. The other two apartments in that building were empty."

"Just me there, huh? What a lucky guy."

"You certainly were lucky I found you in time," Darren added gently.

Alex flushed. "You're right. I don't mean to sound ungrateful. Thank you so much for saving my life. I can never repay you."

"I don't need repayment. I just need to make sure you're okay."

"I am, thanks to you." He paused, feeling like the

words weren't enough, but right now, they were all that he had. He took a sip of water. It helped his raw throat a little. "Do you know how the fire started?"

"Not yet. Not officially. The fire marshal will be doing an investigation. But from my guess, the fire started on the second floor."

"Arson?" Maybe he'd watched too many thrillers, but that worry had been lingering in the back of his mind.

"I don't think so," Darren replied. "Most of the time it's some kind of electrical fire." He paused and glanced at the ceiling as if thinking. "Listen, do you have a place to stay?"

"I'm afraid not. I'm only in Chicago for a show. I was renting that apartment for a month, and then I'd be leaving again."

Darren raised his eyebrows. "What kind of show? Are you some kind of actor?"

Alex laughed and then winced at the burst of pain from his throat and lungs. He was going to have to take it easy until his werewolf genes could finish healing him. "I wish I was an actor. But no, I'm a professional photographer. A freelancer mostly. A gallery was showing some of my work. I shoot both in digital and film. I use a full-frame DSLR. Usually a Canon Mark IV. But sometimes I shoot in standard film or black and white to change things up and focus on the light quality…"

He trailed off when he sensed Darren wasn't that interested in hearing about the intricate details of photography. Alex had seen it lots of times before with people. It wasn't anything overt, just a bit of a blank look that came into people's eyes when Alex went on about composition or light or high-end cameras. He was used to it. He actually should've known better.

"Sounds complex." Darren leaned back in his chair, rubbing along his strong jaw. "You'll have to show me some of your work."

Alex's heart lifted before he realized he'd lost his laptop. "I'd love to…but I lost just about everything in the fire."

"I'm sorry," Darren said. "If you don't have a place to stay, you can stay with me after they release you from the hospital."

Alex flinched, his eyes widening. Another electric thrill shot through him, but he managed to hide it. The offer had caught him by surprise. But as much as he wanted to agree, he knew living with Darren would be a hell filled with constant temptation if Alex's wolf kept insisting the big firefighter was his mate. It would be like having the best ice cream sundae in the world right in front of him, but he'd be unable to gorge himself on it.

In other words, it would be torture.

"Thank you," he said slowly as he searched for the right words. He didn't want to offend Darren. Especially since he was so generous. "That's a very kind offer. But I can stay in a hotel for a few nights. At least until another assignment comes through. So it's not necessary—"

"It *is* necessary," Darren insisted. There was such power and authority in the man's voice that Alex immediately sat up straighter, knowing that refusing had suddenly not become an option. "You need a place. I have a spare room. It's simple."

"Look, you've already done enough. I mean, you saved my life. I don't want to be a charity case—"

"I'm not going to take no for an answer," Darren said, his words half a growl. He leaned forward, pinning Alex with the intensity of his gaze. "Besides, what kind of alpha would I be to let my mate stay in some hotel room and not by my side?"

Darren stood, holding Alex's gaze as Alex's heart went right into his throat and his mind reeled. "It was good meeting you, Alex. I'll be back. Count on it."

Before Alex could reply, Darren nodded to him once and walked out of the room without a backward glance.

Alex lay there on the bed, breathing fast, his heart still pumping hard, feeling like he'd just fallen off a train.

His head was spinning, and he felt almost punch drunk. This morning, the world had been sane. Tonight, everything was crazy. He'd nearly died in a fire. Then he'd met his mate.

Crazy.

"Our mate means to claim us," Alex's wolf insisted joyfully.

"Shut up, you," he thought back at the wolf. *"You're not helping."*

But he couldn't deny the powerful excitement that went shot through his body at the thought of staying with Darren.

Besides, he really didn't have anywhere else to go...

CHAPTER THREE

Darren was there in his big Ford F150 the day Alex was released from the hospital.

He had to refrain from feeling smug. He'd left his number with the nurse's station so Alex could call him. Alex had given in and called him, asking to be picked up in a voice that wasn't exactly meek but did sound a little unsure.

Well, Darren's job was to make Alex sure. His mate would want for nothing. Darren intended to care for him, protect him, and see that his every need was met. It was a raw, primal urge within Darren that wouldn't be denied. Humans might believe he was moving too fast, but things were different for wolves and true mates.

Besides, sometimes you just knew. When he looked at Alex, looked into the omega's kind blue eyes, Darren *knew*.

There were other urges inside him that were making their demands known too, urges he found hard to deny. Such as right now, waiting in the hospital lobby as the elevator doors rumbled open and Alex was pushed out in a wheelchair by an attendant.

The sight of Alex rocked him like a thunderbolt. His wolf insisted he walk over there and drag the other man into a kiss in front of everyone. Claiming him for all to see. His cock was growing thick and hard, wanting far more than just a kiss. It was difficult to think straight with the powerful, raw need racing through him.

He used all his focus and discipline to keep himself under control as he sauntered over to Alex.

Alex smiled when he saw Darren. That was a sweet smile. But sweet as it was, it set Darren's heart pounding faster than a ten-mile run.

How did this other man have such a powerful effect on him? Just a smile had Darren wanting to go down on one knee and propose—either that or sling the omega over his shoulder again and carry him off somewhere private. Somewhere private where Darren could fuck the man until his mate was pleasure-dazed and exhausted from his orgasms.

He cleared his throat and put on a smile that wouldn't reveal exactly how he was feeling right then. "Good to see you, Alex."

"Good to see you too." Alex gestured at his wheelchair. "I'm embarrassed that they're making me use this. I told them I've been on my back enough these last couple of days, but they say it's hospital policy." He met and held Darren's gaze. "I told them I was fine. Thanks to you."

The man's simple gratitude warmed Darren's heart. It made him happy. It was a feeling he knew he could easily get used to.

But he only nodded as if saving Alex's life was no big deal.

"My ride's in the parking lot," he said, knowing that sounded a bit silly. How else had he driven here to pick Alex up? Alex climbed out of the wheelchair and fell into step beside him as they headed for the hospital exit.

Darren towered over the other man, who had to be maybe five-eight, five-nine. He was also almost twice as wide as the lean little omega. But this only made him feel even more protective of the other wolf. The man was so small, he needed a protector. Darren was more than man enough for the job.

Outside, the air was crisp, almost cold with the chill of early autumn in Chicago. Darren led Alex to where he'd parked his truck.

As soon as Alex saw it, he laughed.

"I guessed it right," the omega said, grinning. "You drive a truck."

He smirked. "Firefighters love trucks."

"I can believe that. Besides, with those huge shoulders of yours, I doubt a little electric car would do."

"Could you see me in one of those tiny cars, all squished inside?" he said with mock seriousness. "I'd need a drum of Vaseline to squeeze back out."

Alex laughed again, his eyes sparkling. Those eyes were a pretty shade of blue. They were quite entrancing. Soft, warm, filled with humor. But there was also a bit of a blush on Alex's cheeks.

Darren wondered at that blush until he guessed it must have something to do with the Vaseline quip. Was his little mate having naughty thoughts? If so, Darren encouraged them. He was having quite a few of his own after all.

After Alex was inside and buckled up, Darren took him to the Des Plaines suburbs where he owned a small house. Nothing fancy. A little, three-bedroom tract house that was good enough for him since he lived alone.

Traffic was a bit rough, but he made decent enough time. They made small talk as he drove. Alex certainly lived a life where he got around. Darren had never been out of the country, much less to the Sahara Desert or the rainforests of Brazil. He was impressed.

He finally pulled into the driveway and parked. They both got out.

"This is it," he said to Alex. "It's not much, but it's home."

Alex put his hands on his hips and glanced the place over. "Looks great. I'm always crashing in small, furnished places. Mostly apartments. And they usually have furniture from 1968. Either that or hotels. After a while, all hotels look the same to me. Even in other countries, there's just something so impersonal about them…" He trailed off with a shrug.

Darren looked at him, frowning. "You don't have a home? I assumed you had some kind of home base you went back to. That you were only staying in that apartment in Chicago because you were in town for business."

Although, honestly he hadn't thought about it much. Now that he did, it didn't make much sense. If he had a home somewhere, he would've just stayed at a hotel instead of renting a furnished apartment for a month. But at the time, he'd been more focused on getting Alex to come stay with him after the fire than worrying about someplace else in the country the omega might be living.

Alex shrugged. "My work doesn't really lead to me staying in one place for long. That means no permanent digs. No pets. Just living light on my feet, ready to travel."

Darren let it go even though he wanted to press the man on it. He found it a strange concept. It seemed odd not to have roots somewhere.

But now wasn't the time to go into it. He wanted to get Alex settled in first. Then he could set about convincing Alex that he belonged here with him. After all, an omega deserved to be with his alpha and his mate. And since he didn't have a place and Darren had a perfectly good house, it seemed like the perfect fit.

He led Alex inside. Darren wasn't much for decorating. Yeah, he had the big screen television and expensive sound system. Leather furniture and all of that. He even had an old pinball machine. The walls were mostly bare though. The place was rather sparse. He spent a lot of his time at the fire station. He'd never even really thought about it until now.

The house tour was short and to the point. He showed Alex the bathroom, the kitchen, the laundry room, and the guest bedroom that had a futon in it and a bunch of his free weights. He moved most of the things off to the side and shifted some boxes out of the way.

"I can give you some clean clothes to wear," he said. "They'll be big on you, but it's something until I can get you to the store."

"Thank you…" Alex paused, watching him. "That's generous."

Darren shrugged that off. It wasn't any big deal. "Are you hungry?"

"Not really, thanks. Although I'd like to take a shower."

"I'll get you a towel and some of those clothes. Then I'll take you somewhere you can buy some clothes and a toothbrush or whatever."

"Sounds good. And maybe we could stop at a grocery store? Since you're letting me stay here, I'd like to at least cook you a few meals." He gave Darren an almost shy smile. "I'm pretty good at it."

"Sure," Darren replied, liking the sound of that. "I mostly just grill stuff. I have to warn you. I eat a lot."

"Then I'll make a lot to eat."

They stood there for a second, both of them grinning at each other. It made sense that he would have a good bond with his mate, but part of him was surprised at how easily everything seemed to be falling in place.

"Um…" Alex said, chuckling a little. "If you'll

loan me a towel, I'll get this shower out of the way. And then we can go."

"Right." He went to the linen closet and grabbed a towel and handed it over.

Alex went into the hall bathroom to take his shower. That was where Darren had been taking a shower for the last couple of weeks since he was doing a little remodeling of the master bathroom.

While Alex showered, Darren paced in the living room. His wolf was feeling restless with Alex so close but out of sight.

No, that wasn't right exactly. Darren was restless because Alex was so close and naked in the shower. If his wolf had its way, Darren would burst through the door and jump into that shower with him. He'd pin Alex up against the wall as hot water sprayed on them. He'd soap Alex up, running his hands over that tight little ass, then he'd grab his cock and—

Was it hot in here or what? It shouldn't be this warm in the house in autumn. This was crazy. He needed to get a grip on himself. And that was a double entendre if he'd ever heard one.

He sighed and went to get himself some coffee. He might be hot under the collar, but he desperately needed a distraction. He needed to do something with his hands and take his mind off the sound of the shower and the knowledge that his mate was naked in his house while the powerful urge to claim him raced through Darren's blood.

Darren wasn't sure how long he could play this game. He'd never felt temptation this strong. His wolf was barely under control.

He needed to slow down. Alex had only just been released from the hospital. Even with his werewolf constitution, he still needed to recover. Needed time to adjust.

Growling to himself, he paced into the kitchen and set about making himself some coffee. But it wasn't much of a distraction. The entire time he kept thinking about Alex. How much he wanted to capture the man's lips with his own.

How much he needed to claim him.

* * *

Alex chose to make bruschetta, an antipasto made of grilled bread, veggies, garlic, basil, and tomatoes. For the main dish, he went simple with a classic lasagna. That way he could add a little more meat—ground beef and Italian sausage—which he knew would please Darren. He'd chosen it because he loved Italian food. Also, it was probably the kind of dish Darren didn't get often living alone. Most men were poor or indifferent cooks. Well, except for grilling meat on a barbecue.

After traveling so much, Alex had eaten a lot of wildly different foods. He loved cooking, and he loved feeding people. There was something comforting about doing it. He also loved the conversation, relationships, and interactions when people sat down together for a good, filling meal. People made connections over food. They'd done so for thousands of years, in all kinds of cultures.

Was this his way of trying to thank Darren for all he had done? Or was he trying to find his way to Darren's heart through his stomach?

Now those were really good questions. He didn't have the answer yet.

While Alex cooked, Darren was sitting out on the back deck at Alex's request. Silly as it might seem, Alex didn't enjoy people watching him cook. He loved cooking, but being watched made him nervous, as if he were being judged. Guess that meant a life as a celebrity television chef was out of the question. If it hadn't been for his powerful attraction to Darren, maybe things would've been different. But right now, he felt too self-conscious to cook while Darren watched him. He'd only make mistakes, and he wanted this to be perfect.

But Darren hadn't been upset about it. He didn't seem particularly territorial about his kitchen either, which was good. Sometimes alpha wolves could be over the top about everything.

True to his word, Darren had taken him shopping to one of those big box superstores for new clothes. He'd been right about his clothes being far too big for Alex to wear. He'd had to settle on a huge T-shirt with Darren's fire district insignia on it, rolled up sweatpants, and a Chicago Cubs hoodie. But Darren had paid for all the clothes at the store until Alex could pay him back. Then they'd gone to the supermarket for the ingredients Alex needed for the meal. On the way back, Darren let him use his cell phone to call the bank and get a new bank card rushed out so he would have access to some money. The card was due to arrive tomorrow, delivered to Darren's address. At last, Alex would feel a little less dependent.

He finished putting the final touches on the antipasto and checked the lasagna in the oven. It would probably be done in about twenty minutes.

He fixed up two plates with the bruschetta and balanced them with one arm like a waiter. With his free arm, he grabbed two more cold bottles of beer from the fridge and brought everything out to the deck.

Darren was leaning back in a chair with his feet up on the wooden deck railing. He had a beer in his hand as he watched the sunset-colored clouds changing shades as the evening went on.

Alex tried not the think of how rugged and handsome the man looked. That was too much of a distraction. Those kinds of thoughts always stirred up his inner wolf…and stirred up something else too. Because he wanted the other man so badly it was like an ache. If he let himself stand their stunned and drooling over how strong and sexy Darren was, it would only encourage Alex's omega side. The wolf would go on and on about their mate, and it would drive Alex nuts.

"Another beer?" Alex asked, holding one out temptingly.

Darren nodded and took the cold bottle. Then he tapped his bottle softly against Alex's beer in a toast. "To second chances."

Alex snorted. "Don't you mean, 'to starting over?' Because that's what's in my future."

"To starting over then," Darren amended. His gaze settled on the plates heaped with food that Alex had brought out. "I smell lasagna. What else did you make?"

"Bruschetta. It's great."

Darren looked a little dubious. "Sounds fancy."

"Not really. It's just different. Go on, be brave. Try

it."

"Now you just called me out, so I can't back down." Darren set his beer aside and took a bite of the bruschetta. His eyes widened. "That's good."

Alex grinned. "Told you." He settled into a nearby deck chair and began to eat. "We have twenty more minutes on the lasagna."

They ate in silence for a while, sitting together on the deck. The silence could've been awkward, but Alex was surprised to find it wasn't. He didn't understand why he felt such peace when he was around this man he barely knew, but he couldn't deny it either.

The evening was cool but not too cold. It wasn't quiet really. He could hear traffic and other city sounds, barking dogs and distant music, but Darren's backyard did seem a little world unto its own even in this suburb. The grass was cut, the trees and hedges trimmed. Nothing fancy but clearly well-cared for.

Darren set his bowl aside when he finished. "If the rest of this meal is as good as that was, I'm in for a treat."

"You're in for a treat then," Alex replied, flushing a little with pleasure. That a simple compliment could mean so much to him said a lot. He had it bad. "Because it should be even better. And I made plenty. Even enough for a man your size."

Darren laughed. "Good. I work hard and working

hard makes for a big appetite."

When the oven timer went off, Alex glanced at Darren. "Want to eat inside or out here?"

"How about out here? There aren't many days left before it'll be too cold to sit outside and enjoy it."

"Sounds like a plan." He went inside, found some more plates, and dished out the lasagna. He brought the plates, silverware, and napkins out with him through the French doors onto the deck.

"Smells delicious," Darren said, sitting forward eagerly.

"I hope so." Not all the ingredients had been as fresh as he would've liked, but he'd made do. He desperately wanted Darren to like the food.

Darren began to dig in. He let out a groan and tilted his head back a little. "God, that's damn good."

The sound of Darren's groan had gone right from Alex's ears to shoot straight down to his cock. He tried to get a hold of himself and ignore the sudden surge of lust that went with it. But he couldn't lie. He wanted to hear Darren making that sound again.

And again. And again.

To give himself a chance to regain control and hide how that groan had affected him, he began to scarf down the food. It wasn't bad. He could taste some of the flaws, mostly that the herbs and spices weren't the freshest, but it was edible.

Better yet, Darren seemed to like it. He even went back for seconds. Then thirds.

After they'd eaten, they both enjoyed another beer together. It had felt so comfortable eating with the firefighter that now he felt relaxed, his hunger sated. Right now he felt peaceful and easy. Even thoughts of his desperate situation and not having a place to stay failed to shroud everything in worry again. Alex found himself curious about the other man, eager to know more about him. He was certainly generous and strong, but what else was he like?

"So," he said after a sip of his beer. "What made you become a firefighter?"

Darren leaned back and stretched. "Short answer or long answer?"

"Long answer."

"I like saving people. Protecting people. We do emergency response, so sometimes we're on scene faster than paramedics. Humans don't have all our healing powers, so that makes me protective of them." He paused, thinking. "And the adrenaline. That's part of it too. The danger and the challenge." He shrugged. "We don't always talk about that element, but it's there. Even if we're taking on a fire in an empty structure, trying to knock it down, get it under control, there's still that fight, the challenge of something dangerous."

Alex laughed a little and shook his head. "Wow. It sounds exciting, but it's too dangerous for me. I'd be scared to death."

"It can be scary. That's true. Firefighters aren't crazy. No one wants to be burned. No one has a death wish."

Alex nodded, thinking back to his experience in the burning building. The thick, choking smoke. The fear and the heat. Thinking he was going to die. His respect for Darren deepened even more.

The man was a hero. It was a little intimidating. The most heroic thing Alex could do was take a picture when something exciting was happening. Or maybe cook pasta to perfection. And he was really good at Frisbee golf for some reason. That was about it. He watched the world through a lens, while Darren was out there changing it and saving lives.

He took another sip of his beer. "I admire you."

Darren glanced at him and shrugged again, seeming almost embarrassed by the sudden praise. "I guess I don't think about it all that much. I don't really stand out from the other guys. We're a team. None of us could do it on our own. Humans or shifters, we're all dedicated to our job."

"See? And that's why I admire you. You don't

even make a big deal about what you do. Not everyone can do what you do, believe me."

Darren smiled and tipped his bottle at him. "So enough about me. What about you? Why do you have such a footloose existence?"

Alex leaned back in his chair, gathering his thoughts. "I came from a small town. I guess that made me want to see the world."

"Yeah, I guess I can understand that." Darren leaned forward a little, an earnest expression on his face. "But don't you miss having somewhere you call home?"

"My home is wherever I hang my hat. People get so caught up in having lots of things. They get so caught up in getting more stuff that those things trap them. Stop them from traveling and meeting new people. I don't have that problem."

"Would you ever settle down?" Darren's gaze was sharp. There was a bit of his alpha power behind his words.

Alex could only shrug. "Right now? Honestly, I'm mostly focused on trying to pick up the pieces of my life."

"I can help you with that."

Alex turned to meet his eyes. "Thanks, but…why would you? I'm not trying to be a jerk, but you don't even know me."

"You're my mate. Our wolves know each other. The rest is just filling in the blanks."

Alex bit his cheek to keep from replying with what he wanted to say. Mostly that he didn't believe in all that mate stuff, despite his wolf. Right now he was falling for a guy who saved his life. His hero. Those kinds of feelings were understandable. His wolf was an easily influenced omega, so he wasn't surprised that it was head over heels for a sexy guy like Darren.

"Well…" he said uncomfortably. "I guess. But you've done more than enough already. Tomorrow I'm getting a new bank card so I can pay you back for these clothes."

Darren waved a hand as if it didn't matter at all.

But it did matter to Alex. He wanted Darren to know he appreciated it. But he didn't know how this was going to end. He didn't like to be tied down. He rarely lived in one place for more than three months. His wolf might be ready to bend over for Darren and give up their roaming lifestyle forever, but the human part of Alex wasn't ready.

Maybe would never be ready…

He decided to change the subject, but the only thing he could think of was Darren and his alpha wolf ways. God, he had it so bad for the man, it was crazy. "So…you're an alpha. I can sense it. But why don't you have a pack?"

Darren took so much time to answer that Alex began to fear he'd insulted the man. But finally, he did answer.

"I had a chance to take over a pack in Buffalo about a half-dozen years ago. But a close friend of mine went for it before I made up my mind. It was either challenge him and fight or leave New York. I wasn't about to fight a friend. I'm not that kind of alpha. So I decided I'd move to Chicago, knowing I'd start my own pack from the ground up someday."

"Have you started?" Alex asked. "I mean, finding wolves for your pack?"

Darren gave him a slow, cocky grin. "I just started in fact. I have one in mind right now."

Alex felt heat flare on his cheeks. He had to look away from that confident smile. The man was so sure of himself. Alex wasn't sure of anything anymore…

They sat together until they finished their beers. It was full dark out and getting cold now. By unspoken agreement, they both headed inside. Alex carried the plates into the kitchen and put them in the sink. He got out the dishpan to clean the dishes he'd used, but Darren told him he'd handle it. The cook didn't clean, that was Darren's rule—something taken from the firehouse.

After that, Alex realized he was quite tired. Maybe

he hadn't fully recovered from his stint in the hospital yet, but he was suddenly feeling exhausted.

Darren, sensing the fatigue that came up on Alex so suddenly, walked him to the guestroom and leaned against the doorjamb. His gaze was sharp, intense. Alex couldn't help but notice how much his arm muscles bulged when he folded them across his chest.

"Thanks again for cooking," he said. "It was really good. I haven't eaten that well at home in I don't know how long."

Alex laughed. "I'm glad you enjoyed it. I had a good feeling about how it turned out after you had three helpings."

They stood there smiling at each other. Then Alex's wolf piped up.

"Take our mate to bed," his wolf said in his mind.

He flinched and felt his smile fade. *"Behave yourself. We just met him."*

The wolf might be omega, but once it had something it wanted in mind, it could be surprisingly persistent. And obnoxious. It grumbled and whined and made clear it only wanted to submit to Darren—the sooner, the better—so Darren would take him, claim him.

Alex wanted a little more in life than a one-night fling. He wasn't averse to having fun, hell no. But he found himself wanting to make this other man respect him. He was going to wait and let Darren take the lead…if that was what the man really wanted.

Darren nodded at the guest bed. "Get some sleep. We can talk again in the morning."

Alex yawned. "You're right. I'll make pancakes or something."

"Sounds great, but I hope you like to get up early."

Alex had to bite back a groan. He wasn't an early riser. Never had been. "As long as there's coffee, I should be able to survive."

Darren left after assuring Alex that his bedroom was just down the hall.

That set off Alex's wolf again, making it get all excited and go on about their mate until Alex finally calmed it down.

Finally Alex climbed into bed, sleeping naked in cool, clean sheets. His cock was standing at attention, throbbing with need.

He frowned at it and lay there with his hands laced behind his head. He tried to stare at the ceiling, thinking of baseball or washing dishes or anything that would take his mind off Darren. Take his mind off the way the man looked. How his voice sounded. The incredibly tempting scent of the other shifter…

It took a very long time for Alex to finally fall

asleep. And as he should've guessed, he dreamed about Darren.

CHAPTER FOUR

Darren had a hard time falling asleep. His mind kept returning to the omega sleeping in his guest bedroom. And when he finally did fall asleep, the alarm seemed to wake him five seconds after his eyes closed.

First of all, last night he'd kept wanting to kick down the guestroom door, throw Alex on the bed and cover him with kisses, working the other man's cock until he buckled and shot his seed everywhere with a cry that would be music to Darren's ears. But he managed to restrain himself. Barely.

He doubted the little omega was ready for Darren to shoulder his way into the room and claim him. Not yet anyway. He wasn't sure the other man had fully accepted that they were mates yet.

Darren's wolf was certain. His human side found Alex intriguing and attractive. The desire was easy, shown by the rock-hard erection Darren had sported for half the night. But so far things had been a little frustrating. He hadn't even had a good wet dream about the omega yet. Of course, all of that only made Darren want him even more.

Not only did he want to get Alex into his bed, he also wanted to get to know the man better. He was so different from Darren in so many ways. It was fascinating. Darren had hated leaving New York behind, but he'd also worked hard to build a little family for himself here in Chicago. He was close with the other guys at the station. They were like family to him, especially his friend Mack. But he wanted more. He'd never admitted it aloud to anyone, but he wanted more. He wanted to share his house with a true family. A mate he loved and who loved him back. Children he adored. The whole nine yards.

So he couldn't see living or even enjoying Alex's life of constant travel. It was like having no roots, like being a stick caught in a river current. It would never be the life for him.

He rolled out of bed and stretched with a groan. He pulled on some boxer shorts over his bare ass and headed for the hall bathroom. That's where he had to shower recently because he was replacing the fixtures and repairing some tile work in the house's master bath. He didn't think anything of it when he went inside the hall bathroom and turned on the shower, blinking in the bright overhead lights as he let the water heat up.

He needed to get down to the station this morning. He wasn't on rotation, but he had some paperwork to fill out. He didn't like to let the paperwork pile up. Besides, the guys would want to know that Alex was safe. Everybody took an interest in the people they saved.

Quickly, he shucked off the boxers and stepped into the shower. The shower had frosted glass panels that he intended to replace at some point, maybe after he finished redoing the master bath.

He began to soap himself up, leaning into the hot water, his mind a blank as he lost himself in the simple sensation of water running over his body.

After he was clean, he turned off the water. He was sliding the shower door open, ready to get out, when the bathroom door opened and there was Alex. The omega wolf had hair wildly tousled from sleep and was blinking and squinting in the light.

Seeing him surprised Darren. He froze, wondering why the man was up so early. Also…had Darren really forgotten to close the door behind him? It was entirely possible. He definitely hadn't locked it. He lived alone and had never paid much attention to that before.

Alex finally seemed to notice Darren standing stark naked in the shower. Alex's eyes went very, very wide. His mouth dropped open. His gaze traveled down Darren's chest, lower, sliding down to his cock. Now the omega's eyes seemed to be bulging from his head in a way that had Darren's ego standing up to take notice. Then Alex wrenched his gaze away and forced himself to look Darren in the eyes again.

They both stood there, staring at each other. Time seemed to stand still.

Darren had plenty to enjoy as well. Alex was only wearing a pair of his new boxer shorts they'd bought for him yesterday. His body was as lean and tight as Darren had imagined. He wasn't particularly muscular, but he had a pleasing shape to him that immediately snagged and held Darren's attention. What gripped his attention even more was that Alex was sporting morning wood. His hard cock strained against the fabric of his boxers. He wasn't as big as Darren, but he was big enough to tango with. The urge to touch the man's cock, to stroke it through the thin fabric until it began weeping precum and Alex's head lolled back in pleasure, was so strong it nearly took his breath away.

Alex's face turned bright red. He swallowed with some difficulty. His mouth closed, then opened again. He turned slightly to the side as if trying to hide his erection, but the side view only drew more of Darren's attention to it.

Alex's cheeks seemed to grow even redder. "I…uh. I…umm…"

Darren grinned, suddenly enjoying himself. So he didn't bother to reach for a towel or to hide himself. He liked spurring this reaction in his little omega wolf.

"The door…" Alex continued in a choked voice, getting even redder. "The door was open. I was half asleep. The alarm—your alarm woke me up. I was… I thought I'd make pancakes?" He finished with something more like a question than a statement.

Darren looked him straight in the eye. "I'd love pancakes."

Alex nodded fervently and turned to go.

"Oh, and Alex?" Darren said before the man could finish his retreat.

Alex was looking anywhere but directly at him. But Alex kept throwing little glances at him as if he couldn't look away from Darren's body for long.

"Yes...?"

"Sorry about the alarm waking you. I have it on the loudest setting because I usually sleep like a bear. And don't worry about surprising me." He finally grabbed a towel, but he deliberately began drying his hair, leaving the rest of him exposed. "I forgot to close the door because I'm not used to guests. Sorry about that."

"I... Right. It's...not a problem. I'd better..." He paused and gulped. "I'd better go start breakfast. And coffee. Need coffee."

He practically ran out of the bathroom. Darren managed not to laugh, but he couldn't help grinning to himself. The only reason his little omega mate would be so shy and rattled was because he wanted Darren as badly as Darren wanted him.

As he finished drying off, he realized that it cut both ways. He couldn't get his mind off of Alex. He wanted to go to him in the kitchen and pull him into his arms. He wanted to kiss his way along that delicate neck, nibble at his ears, press his cock against the man's backside. Let the omega know exactly how much Darren wanted him.

But he should probably give the guy a break. He didn't want to come on too strong. Not yet anyway. He didn't want to scare the man off.

Not that Darren intended to let him get away.

Once he was dressed, he wandered into the kitchen. The air was filled with the scent of pancakes and syrup. His stomach growled eagerly. He could certainly get used to this. Having someone cook for him was something he really appreciated. The other thing he really appreciated was Alex's cute little ass in his kitchen.

Alex glanced at him and managed to smile. "Hey, sorry again for this morning. I was stumbling around only half awake. I'm not good until I get some kind of caffeine."

"Don't worry about it," Darren said cheerfully, accepting the mug of coffee that Alex handed him. He took a sip and nodded. It was good, brewed the way he liked. Strong. "Listen, I have to head in to the station today. I have some paperwork to fill out that's going to take a few hours to finish. You're welcome to come, or you can hang out here until I get back."

Alex hid his face behind a sip from his coffee mug, only watching Darren with his beautiful blue eyes over the rim. Then he leaned his head back against the cabinet and sighed. "I'd love to come and see where you work. But I should probably stay here. They're sending a carrier to rush me a replacement card. I'll have to sign for it, I'm sure, and I don't want to miss it."

Darren nodded and shrugged. "No problem. You

aren't missing anything by not watching me fill out paperwork." He grinned. "Paperwork anywhere is boring as hell."

Alex laughed. The intense tension between them lessened a little. It was still there, an ache of desire that he wanted to satisfy and satisfy now. But it had become a little more manageable since both of them were now wearing clothes.

Alex glanced at the stove. "How about some pancakes?"

"I thought you'd never ask," Darren said eagerly.

He sat on a stool at the kitchen island. Alex began to dish out breakfast.

After Darren finally finished stuffing himself with food, he set off for the station. Alex walked him to his truck and waved as he drove away.

Yeah, he could definitely get used to this.

But as he merged onto the highway, headed to work in morning rush-hour traffic, he began to think about other things besides how much he wanted Alex. Thinking about how damn tempting the sight of the man's morning erection had been was a distraction. A nice one, but still a distraction. As much as he hated to admit it, he needed to push back against the constant surge of mating hormones that was clouding his thoughts and emotions.

There was no doubt about it. He needed Alex in his life. He was determined to have him, no matter what. Ever since he'd saved the man, his thoughts had been dominated by the photographer.

But how was he going to make the man his if Alex didn't even live in Chicago? How long would he stay around? Could Darren make him stay? Not by anything crazy like kidnapping or blackmail of course, but could he somehow convince Alex to stay with him and rebuild his life here?

While everything else about Alex seemed so perfect, he was disturbed that the little omega didn't have any roots anywhere. If Alex loved to travel the globe and live in hotels in different cities, how was Darren going to make him his? Had he finally found his mate only to discover they were not perfect for each other after all?

He shook his head and took the exit ramp, heading for the street the fire station was on. No doubt he was getting himself all riled up for nothing. He still had time. He would make his omega see that staying here in Chicago was best. It would make them both happy. That way Alex could rebuild his life into what it was before the fire.

And Darren would be here every step of the way to help him…as long as it meant Alex stayed in his life.

***

Alex's new bank card arrived by courier at eleven o'clock in the morning. He immediately used Darren's phone to call a ride-sharing service to take him to the nearest store selling cell phones. He thought about calling Darren to let him know he was going out but decided against it. He didn't have the man's cell phone number, and he didn't even know what fire station he worked at. There were a lot of fire stations in Chicago. He'd just fill him in when he got back.

It turned out to be a productive trip. He took out cash from his account to repay Darren for the clothes, and he purchased a new cell phone he could buy minutes for since he'd lost his phone in the fire. But at least he could check his email.

Sure enough, there were dozens of messages for him about work. He sorted through them, marking the assignments and photo shoots that would pay the most as the highest priority. Then he called his insurance company and started a claim for his lost camera, laptop, and the rest of his stuff. It didn't amount to much, so he was sure there wouldn't be a big problem with the claim.

When he finally got back to Darren's house, he

was surprised when the man came out of the house to meet him as he was tipping the driver.

Darren waited until the driver pulled away and then frowned at him. "Where were you?"

Alex bristled a little at the demanding tone. "What? Do I suddenly have a leash or something? I got my replacement bank card. I needed to get a few things."

Darren's frown deepened. "You could've called me."

Alex eyed him before pulling out his new cell phone. "No, I couldn't have called you, because I don't have your number."

"You called me from the hospital."

"Darren… I don't have the kind of memory for phone numbers necessary to remember a number I used once. But now I have a cell phone again, and I can put your number in it." He paused, his brow furrowing. "What's wrong? Why is this such a big deal?"

Darren didn't answer right away. He shoved his big hands in his pockets and shook his head. "It's not. I just got worried when I came back and you were gone. The wolf is pretty protective. Sometimes it gets a little out of control."

Alex couldn't help a grin. The big firefighter actually looked contrite.

"Yeah, you're right. I should've thought of that.

But everything's fine. In fact," he said, reaching behind him to take out his new wallet. "I have some money for you." He pulled out enough cash and held it out to Darren. "Thanks again for giving me a little loan so I could buy some clothes. I really appreciate it."

Darren shook his head at the money. "I'm not going to take that money, so you might as well put it back in your wallet." He waved a hand dismissively. "That was a gift. Something to help you out. It wasn't a loan."

"Are you sure…?"

"I'm sure of everything," Darren said, almost curtly. "So I'm definitely sure of this. So thank you for offering to pay me back, but I definitely don't need the money. You should keep it. I know you'll need to replace your equipment. And I'm sure that can be expensive."

Alex smiled. "Thank you. I mean it. And there's good news on that front too. I placed a claim with the insurance company today. I'm not sure how long it will take, but at least with my bank card, I can get started again. Maybe get caught up on work." He held up his cell phone and laughed gently. "I made the mistake of checking my email. Whoa. I have a whole mess to sort out."

Darren seemed a little distant, maybe even disappointed to hear that. But the look was gone from his face almost before Alex could be sure it was there.

"Good to hear," Darren said, his deep voice booming. "Now what do you say we sit down and have a beer after a hard day's work?"

Alex held up one of his shopping bags. "I'd say that's a great idea, but I'd also say that I have some cooking to do first. I'm thinking garlic-crusted prime rib. Lots of meat. But I'll throw in some sauteed mushrooms and creamy mashed potatoes."

Darren tilted his head back and closed his eyes. "You are a gift from heaven."

Alex laughed, but part of him was touched by those words. Even if Darren was kidding around, it did feel good to be needed somewhere. To feel appreciated. He only hoped this dish lived up to expectations.

They went inside Darren's house. Alex headed for the kitchen and began prepping to cook because he could see that Darren was hungry.

Darren followed him in and leaned against one of the counters. "Mind if I watch?"

"Um…I usually cook alone…well, because usually it's just me. And I guess I'm not used to being watched."

Darren shrugged. "I'm not a good enough cook to criticize you, if that's what you're afraid of. But this way I can talk with you."

Alex hesitated. Then he decided he was being an

ass for being so shy and nervous about it. He needed to show Darren he wasn't timid. He was never timid…or at least he'd never been until he'd met Darren. The alpha's raw power and presence seemed to make Alex more hesitant than he'd ever been in his life. But maybe instead of being tentative, he should take a cue from Darren and project confidence. Be bold. Grab life by the horns. Howl at the moon. All of that kind of thing.

Yeah. He liked that.

"Okay, if you want, you can stay. We can talk about how our days went," Alex said, amused. "I can go on about my busy time shopping for toiletries."

"And my busy day filling out safety paperwork and training forms." Darren grinned back. "You'll learn the secret of firefighters everywhere. That firefighter life isn't always as action-packed as it is in the movies."

"What life ever is?" Alex replied gently. "Being a photographer means a lot of waiting around, waiting on the perfect shot. Waiting for the right lighting. Waiting for the right exposure, the right moment. So I know things aren't always as glamorous as they seem from the outside."

He began to cook. At first it was a little awkward for him, because he was very, *very* aware of Darren's presence. The man seemed to command a room just by standing in it. But soon it was clear Darren wasn't judging his cooking skills, so he began to get over himself and relax. He focused on putting the meal together while Darren told stories about life at the fire station.

From the sound of it, the firefighters played a lot of pranks on each other. Also, they all sounded close, like brothers or one big family. Alex actually found himself wishing he had something like that in his life. True, he had friends…but he didn't get to see them all that often because of his travels.

When the meal was finished cooking, they ate on the deck again. Again by unspoken agreement, they both stayed out to enjoy a beer after the meal.

Darren groaned and stretched. "Another excellent meal, Alex. Thank you." He tipped his beer in Alex's direction.

Alex copied one of Darren's shrugs, but he really felt pleased at the praise. Too often he was only cooking for himself, so if he did anything fancy, there wasn't anyone to appreciate it. He'd missed cooking for other people, enjoying meals together, sharing good conversation. This last year had been too hectic by far. Besides, he enjoyed cooking for Darren. And since the man ate so much, it was easy to believe he really enjoyed Alex's cooking.

He stood to clear the plates and head back inside. As he reached for Darren's plate, Darren caught his hand

and held it. The other man's hand was rough and callused. It was strong and warm.

Alex didn't try to pull away. A thrill shot through him, and his heart began to pound faster.

"Do you feel it?" Darren asked, his voice rough and his gaze intense. "The connection between us?"

Alex sucked in a breath. He could only nod slowly. His body was trembling. The big wolf's aura seemed to crash against him, dominating him but also making him feel protected…and desired. He could see the lust in the big man's eyes. It burned there like a blowtorch flame.

Darren wanted him.

Slowly, Alex nodded. He was biting his lip, trying to keep a needy groan from escaping. He didn't know why he was fighting his own desires. He yearned to give in. He wanted Darren to kiss him. He could lose himself in a kiss…

Darren leaned closer to him. "Good. I haven't been able to take my eyes off you since I met you, Alex. You are all I think about."

Alex opened his mouth to reply, but no words came out. His heart was beating even faster, pounding in his chest. The way Darren was looking at him was stirring Alex's cock to life, that tightening need, almost an ache, beginning down in his groin. He had a heat inside him that could only be soothed by Darren's touch. That was the kind of powerful fire the big firefighter set off inside him.

Darren stood slowly. He was big, broad, and strong but he was also graceful. The man was so tall that he looked down into Alex's eyes with an intensity that took Alex's breath away. He shifted his grip from Alex's hand to reach up and cup his jaw, his touch gentle, strong but tender.

He's going to kiss me, Alex thought, amazed. There was nothing he wanted more right now.

Darren seemed to see the desire in Alex's eyes. An almost cocky smile appeared on his lips. He leaned forward, his eyes flashing. Alex tilted his head, offering his lips and closing his eyes.

Darren's kiss rocked him to the core. The intensity of it nearly brought him to his knees. Darren's firm lips claimed his. He pulled Alex tight against him. Alex felt the man's muscular body. He moaned when he felt the press of the man's erection.

Right now he felt like he was on fire from the inside out. His thoughts dissolved into blankness as Darren deepened the kiss. When Darren's tongue pushed past his lips, Alex opened his mouth greedily. His hips began to arch slightly, rubbing his own hard cock against Darren's body. Showing the alpha how turned on he was.

Showing Darren how much he wanted him, needed him right now.

They were both breathing hard and fast when Darren finally ended the kiss. He looked deep into Alex's eyes.

"I'm not going to lie or play games," Darren said in a deep voice that sounded like half a growl. "I want to make love to you, Alex. Hell, I want to fuck you so hard and good that you won't even know your own name when I'm done. I want to make you feel like you've never felt before." His eyes flashed. "Do you want that too?"

At first, words wouldn't come to his lips. He half expected to overheat and swoon at the look in Darren's eyes, at the desire in his words, like he was in some kind of old-fashioned movie. Either that or spontaneously shoot off in his pants and then fall over. He had never wanted anyone as badly as he wanted Darren right then. He was rock-hard, his thoughts fuzzy with his own lust. He felt almost lightheaded, even though he'd only had one beer. He wanted to be loved. He wanted to get out of his own head, put all his worries and fears aside, and simply enjoy one of the best things in life. The touches, the kisses, the love of another very special person.

His voice was steady when he looked into Darren's eyes. "I want that."

Darren's smile was bright enough to light up the darkest cave.

He pulled Alex into another kiss.

They were kissing as they fumbled their way back through the door. He didn't spare a thought for the dishes and beer bottles they left on the deck table. He wasn't going to stop these kisses for anything.

He was barely aware of Darren guiding him down the hall, into the master bedroom. The room was full of Darren's scent, and Alex's wolf whimpered in need. Darren's hands were all over his body, caressing him, gripping his ass, then sliding up his thigh to rub his cock through his pants. The whirlwind of sensations left him dizzy…and greedy. He indulged in his own caresses, feeling the firefighter's rock-hard muscles, his perfect abs, the steel length of his cock straining against those jeans.

Darren practically tore off Alex's shirt, getting it out of the way quickly so he could keep kissing Alex. His skin felt so hot when he caressed his hands up Alex's sides to his chest. One of Darren's thumbs traced idly over Alex's nipple, stimulating it until it pebbled and stood up in a hard, tight nub. A groan of pleasure escaped Alex's lips.

Then Darren was undoing Alex's belt, drawing down his zipper, pushing his pants down, all without stopping kissing him. Alex kicked off his shoes and stepped out of the pants puddled around his ankles, also without breaking their kiss.

The alpha's big hand brushed against Alex's hard cock, skimming along where it tented the cotton of his boxer shorts. That drew a frantic gasp from Alex and had him arching his hips forward, desperate for more of the man's touch.

Instead, Darren gently but firmly pushed him back onto the large bed. Alex was lying there, naked except for his boxer shorts. His legs were slightly spread, his hard length still jutting eagerly against the cotton fabric as he stared up at Darren.

Eyes blazing, Darren began to strip. He yanked his own shirt over his head and tossed it behind him.

God, the man had a perfect torso. His pecs were big, tight slabs of muscle. Those abdominal muscle ridges looked to have edges hard enough to break rocks into gravel. At the sight, Alex's cock twitched, and the desire pooling in his groin was a desperate, needy ache.

Next, Darren kicked off his boots, unbuckled his pants, and slowly slid them down his thighs. He also kicked the jeans aside, and without pause, yanked down his boxer shorts.

Alex bit his lip, his eyes wide. Desperately, he reached down to grip his own cock tightly, using lots of pressure but not moving his hand much. It was a struggle to control himself and not to pump his hand up and down his dick while staring at Darren. But he knew if he did, he would lose it completely.

Darren's gorgeous, naked body was wrapped in muscle, his hard cock jutting out from him, thick, long, surrounded by dark pubic hair and a vein running along the shaft. The tip was dusky red. The slit was wet with precum.

As Alex stared, breathing in short, shuddering gasps, Darren settled a fist around his cock and pumped it. He was doing just what Alex wanted to do but didn't dare. Alex was so aroused right now, he was afraid he would come too soon if he did the same. Instead, he let go of his cock with a shaking hand, desperate to remove the building temptation.

Darren's heated gaze never left Alex. He seemed to drink in Alex's arousal. To revel in it, as if he knew how much the sight of a perfect man stroking a perfect cock turned Alex on.

Alex's urge to fondle his own rock-hard cock was almost too much to deny. But he did deny it, even though his cock was throbbing against his boxer shorts. With trembling hands, he skinned down his silk boxers and tossed them over the edge of the bed.

He glanced at Darren again almost shyly. Alex's

body was lean, and his cock was smaller than Darren's, but the man was watching him with eyes blazing with lust. Something about Alex had certainly heated Darren's blood.

"See what looking at you naked does to me?" Darren growled, a predatory grin on his face as he pumped his long cock with long, slow strokes.

All Alex could do was nod wordlessly. His heart was in his throat. He couldn't seem to tear his gaze away from Darren's body. God, he ached for the man to touch him. And he wanted his lips on Darren's skin, to kiss him everywhere, worshiping that incredible body.

Darren walked over to him and straddled him, pressing his body down on Alex, hot, naked flesh against naked flesh. Alex gasped as their cocks pressed against each other.

With slow, deliberate movements, Darren began to pump his hips, creating decadent pleasure that pulsed through Alex's cock at the silken friction. As if they had a mind of their own, his hips began to pump in time to Darren's. Precum was seeping from the tip of his cock. His body was tense at the incredible sensations gripping him.

Darren pushed himself up the slightest bit, muscles flexing. He reached down between them with one of his big hands and encircled both their cocks in his grip. Not too tightly, but with just enough added pressure to make Alex's eyes roll back and an unsteady gasp to escape his lips.

"Feel good, little omega?" Darren demanded.

His mind couldn't form words. He could only nod as waves of pleasure washed through him.

He hadn't had sex with anyone in a long time. God, he missed this. The building tension in his groin, the pulsing waves of pleasure as they rubbed their cocks together, trapped in Darren's big hand, and he felt like any moment he was going to lose it and explode.

"St-stop…" he gasped. "Or I'm gonna cum all over your hand."

Darren's laugh was a deep rumble. He pumped a couple more times, probably just to torment Alex.

For his part, Alex had to quickly think of bread recipes and the challenges of full-spectrum photography to stop himself from losing it and spurting his hot cum all over Darren's fingers.

With a smug grin, Darren released his grip, but not before sliding his big finger over the tip of Alex's cock. His thumb came away wet with Alex's precum. Darren lifted his finger to his mouth, grinned, and licked it clean.

Alex knew that if he'd been standing, his knees would've given out. He wanted nothing more than to lie back on the bed and spread his legs for Darren, allowing him access to anything he wanted. He just wanted Darren's big cock to fill him, to penetrate him deep…

After a deep, passionate kiss, Darren rolled off him. Alex immediately missed his touch, his body heat.

Darren stood and reached for the nightstand. He brought out a tube of lubricant. But before he could open it, Alex sat up off the bed.

He wanted to give Darren something to remember too. He wanted to make the man who'd saved his life feel absolutely incredible.

So he sank down on his knees before Darren, almost as if worshiping him. He reached out a trembling hand and slid it down the length of his shaft. Slowly, teasingly, he began to stroke down the man's big shaft. With his other hand, he skimmed his hand under Darren's ball sack, feeling the hair brush against his skin. His stroke was light, but it had Darren gritting his teeth as if he was fighting to keep control.

He leaned forward and took Darren's hard length into his mouth. Darren's hands moved to Alex's head as Alex began to move his mouth up and down on his cock. Alex groaned at the taste of the other shifter, and the vibration of his groan made Darren's body go rigid, and his hands tighten in Alex's hair.

It seemed like the alpha liked what Alex was

doing.

"All right, damn it," Darren said in a rough voice. "You're too good at that."

Darren gently but firmly moved back, pulling his cock from Alex's mouth.

"I'll take that as a compliment," Alex said. He licked his lips, grinning up at the big man.

Darren saw the grin and chuckled. "It was. But now it's my turn."

He drew Alex to his feet and rocked him on his heels with another mind-blowing kiss. Then he dragged Alex to the edge of the bed, leaving him on his back, and pushed his legs up. Alex was breathing fast, his cock throbbing. He tilted his hips, presenting himself for Darren.

Now Darren took up the lube again. He never looked away from Alex as he filled his hand, then coated his dick with lube. Alex watched him greedily, nearly whimpering with his need to be filled. He knew what was coming next, and he was looking forward to it with all his heart.

Next, Darren poured more lube into his hand. He carefully, gently coated Alex's hole with a slick finger. Then he slowly worked the lube in, teasing the tight muscle until Alex began to relax. He slipped in one finger, then a second, giving Alex time to adjust. Alex closed his eyes, feeling the pressure of Darren's fingers, the slight burn, then adjusting to him. Again carefully, Darren began to slide his fingers in and out, opening him even further.

When Alex was ready and biting his lip against the wonderful sensations traveling through his body, Darren shifted position until he was lined up. He grabbed the base of his cock with one hand, the other pushing back Alex's leg. The large head of his cock pressed at Alex's hole.

Alex watched with wide eyes as Darren pressed forward, his slick cock pushing past the muscle. Slowly, he eased it in deeper as Alex's eyes closed and he leaned his head back to better focus on the sensation of being slowly filled.

When Darren was all the way in, he paused, letting Alex's body adjust to his width. After Alex met his eyes and nodded, Darren began to fuck him. Slowly at first. Long, deep, slow strokes.

Then Darren shifted his right hand from holding Alex's leg. He leaned forward to grip Alex's cock. The angle change made Alex moan with pleasure. The hand on his cock made him moan even more. Had anything in the world ever felt as good as this? He didn't care about anything else. All his thoughts, all his worries had evaporated from his mind.

Darren mercilessly worked Alex's shaft even as he increased the speed of his thrusts. Alex's eyes rolled back in his head when Darren fucked him even harder, plunging deep, his hand working Alex's cock relentlessly.

The orgasm built so fast that he barely had time to suck in a breath and let out a cry of pleasure. His body transformed into perfect fire, an explosion of bliss, a fucking orgasm that rocked him to his core. An orgasm that had him arching his back, his cock pulsing as he shot his cum onto his chest and stomach. His seed was so warm it burned against his skin. Darren slowed his pumping hand on Alex's cock as Alex rode the orgasm out. His whole body was trembling from the force of it.

But even as Darren released his cock, he began to pound Alex even faster. Now that he'd gotten Alex off, he was ready to come too.

There was nothing Alex wanted more. He watched Darren's rugged face, enraptured, as the man thrust into him, shaking the entire bed.

It wasn't long before Darren's perfect body went tense. He drove all the way in and gripped Alex's ass tight, lifting him from the edge of the bed and holding him aloft as his cock began to spurt his cum deep inside Alex.

It was one of the most stunning things Alex had

ever seen.

After Darren came down from his orgasm, he slowly opened his eyes and grinned down at Alex. Alex smiled back with a dazed, sated smile that showed how happy and content he was right then.

Darren withdrew from him slowly, making sure not to hurt him. They were both breathing fast. Darren leaned over him, nipping at his neck with his teeth, marking him. Then he kissed his way up Alex's jawline to claim his lips with a last kiss.

Alex closed his eyes and gave himself to the kiss, barely having enough energy to kiss back. Darren ended the kiss and scooped Alex up as if he weighed nothing. He gently set him down again in the center of the bed. Then he climbed in beside him.

Greedily, Alex snuggled against him. He loved the silken, warm feeling of the alpha's skin. He loved the scent of him. And inside, his wolf was howling with happiness. He rested his head against Darren's chest, already drifting off to sleep, completely sated.

"Are you happy, my little mate?" Darren asked, his voice a rumbling sound like thunder.

"Yes…" he murmured sleepily, just enjoying how he felt. Enjoying the sound of Darren's voice. He didn't want this night to end, but he was drifting off to sleep, safe in the arms of the alpha who'd saved his life…

CHAPTER FIVE

Alex woke before dawn after a night that had started out great but ended up being a mostly sleepless one. He'd woken again about two a.m. and hadn't been able to drift off again. Darren had slept well beside him, never waking once. Alex was jealous, but his brain had been full of thoughts that had relentlessly kept him awake.

As mind-blowing, as amazing as the sex had been, he came to the realization that he'd made a mistake.

This should never have gone this far. Now his wolf was insisting that Alex give up everything and stay here with Darren forever. And had his brain melted at some point when his desire and hormones had been raging? Because he also realized Darren had used plenty of lube but no protection. Normally it wasn't a big deal because he was a shifter with all a shifter's resistances. But with an alpha? *That* was a big deal.

So mistakes on top of mistakes. Now his wolf was yipping at him to settle down for good.

He wasn't a kept man—or a kept omega. He had too much self-respect for that. It was clear from yesterday that Darren—or at least his wolf—believed they had some kind of claim on Alex. That much was clear. He couldn't even blame Darren. The man was an alpha wolf. That was what alphas did.

But now Alex had to decide what he wanted to do. Darren had been extremely generous. Alex owed him everything, including his life. So that made his second thoughts feel almost traitorous. He should be grateful for everything Darren had done. And he was grateful. That was what made this so hard…

No. He had to ignore his wolf's submissive impulses and do what was best for the human part of him.

He couldn't stay here with Darren in Chicago. His omega wolf might disagree, but he was more than just his wolf and those omega instincts. He was better than that. He had hopes and dreams and desires to fulfill. Staying here with Darren was just too tempting. He could see himself staying and setting down roots. He could imagine cooking for Darren every night and sharing his bed every night as well. The thought was so alluring it was almost an ache inside him.

But being a kept omega wasn't him. It never had been. He wasn't ready to give up his life of adventure and travel, even for love.

Even for Darren.

He didn't shower. He felt the guilt weighing around his neck as he crept out of the room and ever so gently shut the door behind him. He used his cell phone to call a cab, then gathered up what few things he still had on this earth. He couldn't help himself from taking the T-shirt Darren had loaned him—the one with his station logo on it. He needed something to remember the man by…and a T-shirt would have to do.

Alex quickly scribbled a note on a piece of paper and left it on the counter. It was a cowardly thing to do…but he knew if he stayed here and tried to tell Darren face to face, he'd never have the strength to leave.

Even now, part of him desperately wanted to stay.

The entire time he waited for the cab to arrive, he was on pins and needles. He was sure Darren was going to wake up before he left. He didn't want a big fight. He didn't want to hurt the other man. Especially after what they'd shared. Alex would never forget their time together. How could he? It had been a perfect night.

He prayed that Darren would understand and have no regrets.

But somehow he knew the alpha wouldn't. That broke his heart.

The cab finally arrived. Alex went out to meet it before the guy could honk for him. He closed the front door softly. It felt like he was running away like a coward and he hated that. His wolf was whimpering, already mourning leaving their mate.

He ignored his wolf. He needed to be strong, resolute. He refused to live his life through the instincts of an omega wolf. If he had, he never would've been able to find the gumption to travel the world and make his living with a camera lens. He would've taken some other job that was safe, waiting for an alpha to swoop in and claim him.

Ten minutes later, the cab was on the freeway. Forty minutes after that, he was at Chicago O'Hare. And an hour after arriving, he was in the air, headed to Boston.

He would stay in Boston while he got his passport replaced. As soon as he had a replacement passport, he was headed to Madrid, where he had the chance at a photo shoot in a couple of months that would replenish his bank account and let him get his feet back under him again.

But every single moment away from Darren had him yearning to be back in Chicago, talking with the firefighter who had saved his life.

He gritted his teeth and steeled himself against the emotions all twisted up inside him. His wolf wasn't happy. He wasn't happy. Maybe he'd made another mistake. It certainly hurt enough to be a mistake. But he wasn't ready to settle down and be owned—even with a man as incredible as Darren Drake. The alpha who'd saved his life.

He was afraid he was being selfish, being a coward. But he had cast the dice and made his choice. He would have plenty of time for regrets later.

He looked out the airplane window at the passing clouds. Yes, maybe he'd made a terrible mistake, but it was one he was going to have to live with.

There was no going back now…

* * *

Darren woke up naked and alone on the bed. Frowning, he glanced at the sheets where Alex had slept last night. He could still smell the omega's tempting scent all around him.

He stretched and rolled out of bed. He walked, still naked, from the bedroom, expecting to find Alex in the bathroom or in the kitchen making breakfast.

He was in neither.

That woke him up all the way. He listened closely and scented the air. He couldn't hear anything out of the ordinary, and even though Alex's scent was everywhere now, it was hours old.

He didn't like this. Not one bit. Where the hell could Alex be? Had he gone out to buy breakfast or coffee? Was there something he wasn't thinking of?

He walked the house again and then went outside. Still no sign of Alex. But when he came back in, he noticed a piece of paper sitting on the counter. A cold feeling started in the pit of his stomach as he walked over and picked it up.

He scanned the note with his heart in his throat.

Darren,

I can't thank you enough for all you've done. I'll never forget the time we had. But I'm not a guy who can stay in one place. I'm sorry. You deserve better.

Alex

He stood there, staring at the note, unable to believe it. The ache in his chest told him how much pain he was feeling, but he felt strangely disconnected from it. He couldn't think of what could've happened to drive Alex away. They'd seemed to fit together so well. Hell, there was desire, but there was also something more. Something even deeper. How could the bastard deny it? How could he run?

He was angry now. He paced the room with the note in his hand, but he was careful not to crush it. The anger smoldered inside him like a hot coal.

He went to his phone, thinking he could call Alex and demand an explanation. Then he realized that even though Alex had bought a new phone, Darren had never got the omega's new number. He'd meant to…but it hadn't happened. Calling him was out of the question.

He growled in frustration. He paced through the house again, wanting to do something to make this right but having no idea how. His frustration was making him desperate.

Clearly Alex had called a cab to get a ride out of here. How long had he been gone? He'd taken the stuff he'd bought along with him, so it didn't look like he intended to come back.

That fact echoed in his mind like a tolling bell.

Alex wasn't coming back.

Where would he go? He had no problem traveling all over the world, so he would probably head to O'Hare. But Darren had no idea where the other man might fly to from there. Had he lost his passport in the fire? Probably. But that still left plenty of cities Alex could fly to in the U.S. How could a simple guy like Darren track a man who traveled for a living?

He couldn't. He wasn't a spy or some kind of hacker or whatever. Alex knew where he lived, but Darren had no idea how to get in touch with the omega. If Alex never wanted to see him again, Darren wouldn't be able to find him because Alex didn't seem to have a permanent address.

He looked at the clock again. A long, shuddering sigh left his lips. Time was running out quickly. He needed to head into work soon. He was on shift at the fire station for the next few days. He didn't have the luxury of rushing to the airport to try to head Alex off before he made a mistake and boarded a plane.

Darren had responsibilities. He had people counting on him. Alex didn't seem to have any responsibilities. He just went wherever he wanted.

He didn't want to admit it, but maybe this whole thing had been a terrible mistake. His wolf had been so certain he'd found his mate in the omega, but what if he'd been wrong?

The more he thought about it, the more he realized the whole thing was crazy. What did he really have in common with the roaming photographer except for some feelings of desire? Yeah, he felt protective of the omega. Those feelings were very powerful too. But maybe that was just his alpha side rearing its head. He'd saved the man's life. Of course he felt protective of him.

Maybe he'd been a fool. He shook his head and snorted. He'd never thought of himself as a romantic fool before, but if the boot fit…

Fool or not, he had to get to work. His personal life had just gone down in flames, but he wouldn't forsake his job, his duty, or his responsibilities.

Still, as he showered and got ready to head in to the station, he knew he was moving slower than normal, and his thoughts were dark and heavy.

He missed Alex already. Damn the omega for making him feel something for him. Darren missed Alex's smile, his scent, the way his eyes lit up when he talked about his photography or cooking. The way Alex had felt in his arms.

As if he belonged there.

Now that was all gone. Probably for good.

With a heavy heart, he got in his truck and drove to work and tried to put Alex Carson behind him forever.

CHAPTER SIX

Eight months later...
Chicago

Alex maneuvered himself carefully into the seat of the car he'd leased yesterday, sliding the seat back as far as it would go to accommodate his belly. He wasn't a tall guy, but steering wheels always seemed to be a problem since he'd really, *really* started showing.

It was good to be back in Chicago. He'd been here for a week already, taking care of business like leasing a car, finding a furnished place to live, all while trying to get up the nerve to go see Darren again. It seemed like nothing in the city had changed since he'd fled eight months ago. But he felt like he was a completely different person.

Inside him, the baby turned and kicked. He could see the movement clearly outlined against the tight stretch of his shirt. He put his hand on his belly and smiled.

"Hang tight, little guy," he murmured. "It's a big day for both of us."

He knew the baby could sense his nervousness. How could he not? Ever since Alex had returned to Chicago, his heart had been beating faster, his breath was short, his skin colder, and a feeling of dread tumbled around in his stomach like a load of wet clothes in the dryer.

He prayed he was making the right decision.

Alex was going to find Darren Drake. He was going to tell Darren that he was carrying Darren's child. He was an omega, and he was pregnant with the alpha's son.

He had no idea how the firefighter would react. They'd shared an incredible night together months ago. This precious baby was the unexpected result of that. He'd kept the secret to himself for months, with only a few scattered friends around the world knowing. During that time, he'd thrown himself back into his work. He was desperate to rebuild his life after the fire. And after leaving Darren.

But despite everything he'd done, he couldn't seem to fill the hole inside him.

He had not gone a day without thinking of Darren. He had not gone a day without missing the man. Leaving him had been a mistake. One in a long line of mistakes he'd made in his life. Now he was afraid the firefighter would be furious with him for getting pregnant, not to mention for leaving with only a note to say goodbye. Alex was afraid of what Darren would say. Would he call Alex a coward? Curse him for vanishing without a trace?

He would deserve those curses and more.

Still, Darren had a right to know about his child. So he was determined to press on, no matter what.

Sighing, he started the car and turned up the air conditioning. It was an unseasonably warm day in Chicago. Even the wind was hot. He buckled himself in, always something of an amusing, exasperating challenge with his pregnant belly. Then he put Darren's address in the car's GPS map program.

He was going to show up on Darren's doorstep pregnant. He didn't see any way this could end well. But again, he remained determined to go through with it because Darren deserved to know the truth. He also deserved to play a role in his son's life. And yes, the ultrasound had clearly shown that Alex was carrying a boy. Judging from the strengths of his kicks, he was some kind of future ninja or soccer player or maybe even a mule.

Smirking, he pulled onto the road, headed for Darren's house. He turned on the radio, finding a classical music station. He'd heard somewhere that classical music was good for a child's mathematical development.

Even though the music was soothing, his nerves refused to settle. The traffic didn't help either.

When he finally stopped in front of Darren's house, he was immediately hit with a powerful wave of memory and emotions. Moments from their brief time together flashed through his mind like scenes from a movie projector. He sat there in the driver's seat, his hands gripping the wheel so hard that his knuckles were white.

The urge to put the car back in gear and race away was so strong that he barely fought it off. He had to practice his Lamaze breathing technique to settle himself down.

Surprisingly, it worked.

He stared at the house. Darren's truck was in the driveway. That meant he was home. So much for hoping the man was gone so he could put this off for another day.

Now he had no excuse. If he drove off now, it would be pure cowardice. People thought omega wolves were cowardly and timid enough. He wasn't going to feed into that stereotype. Not anymore. He had to set a good example for his son.

Alex opened the car door. Then he managed to heave and lever himself out of the seat. No one really appreciated what a pain low car seats were until they were carrying a watermelon in their abdomen.

Putting a hand on his belly, he murmured, "Come on, kid. We're in this together. Let's go meet your dad."

His baby kicked enthusiastically. Alex winced. It felt like his child was trying to kick his bladder into submission, and that wasn't fun.

He began to walk up the path to the front door, trying not to do the pregnant waddle. He was due in twenty-nine days. By now, he was used to the glances from strangers and used to feeling like a baby-hauling blimp most of the time. He suspected that if more males had to go through this, they'd be a lot more sympathetic of the challenges of pregnancy that women faced. Like having to use the bathroom all the time. Or morning sickness. Or peeing a little if he laughed too hard. That was one of the most annoying things.

When he'd first gone to the doctor two months after leaving Chicago, he'd been just as terrified as he was right now. Deep in his heart, he'd known he was pregnant. His body felt strange, his hormones out of whack, and he was bloated in disturbing ways. He'd gone to a doctor specializing in omega werewolves. The doctor had been so calm and professional that he'd done much to set Alex at ease.

A quick test later, and he'd known for sure.

He was pregnant, and it could only be Darren's baby.

Now the time had finally come to share the news.

He reached the door. After offering a silent prayer to any listening deity, he pushed the doorbell. Being this pregnant, he knew he couldn't run away. One way or another, he was all in.

The door swung open. Darren was right there, staring at him. Shock flashed across his face as his eyes widened in a way that might have been funny in another situation, at another time.

The man was just as handsome as Alex remembered. Dark hair. Intense hazel eyes. Rugged appearance. Jawline that could break rocks. He was wearing a dark blue T-shirt with his fire station insignia on it. The T-shirt fit him like a glove, showing off all those big muscles and those broad shoulders. Alex had to push a memory of running his hands over that godly body out of his mind. He couldn't afford to be distracted right now. But that was easier said than done.

"You," Darren said in a voice that was nearly a growl. Then his gaze dropped down to Alex's bulging belly. "Wait. No way…"

This was what he'd feared. Was Darren going to deny being the father? Right now he looked shocked and angry enough to do anything.

"May I come inside?" Alex asked quietly.

Darren stared at him, saying nothing.

Alex could see the pain and anger in his eyes. Guilt hit him so hard that for a moment he couldn't breathe. His insides tensed up as if he'd suddenly frozen solid, his stomach and lungs encased in ice.

Something seemed to slam down behind Darren's eyes, hiding his emotions behind a purposefully blank face. Instead of answering, Darren turned and walked away, out of the foyer. But he hadn't slammed the door in Alex's face, so Alex took that as an invitation to follow.

He caught up with Darren in the kitchen. The alpha was leaning against the counter with his arms folded across his chest. He stared at Alex as Alex stepped inside.

"I'd offer you a beer," Darren growled, "but in your condition, you can't have one."

"Thanks for pointing that out," Alex snapped, irritated. "I hadn't noticed."

Darren ignored his sass. "Why are you here, Alex?"

Frustration swept through him, and his mouth felt as dry as sand. "I think you know."

"I don't like games. Are you here to say that the kid you're carrying is mine? If so, come out and tell me."

"Fine." He drew himself up, shoulders back, meeting the other man's cool gaze. He put a hand on his belly almost defensively. "This kid is yours."

Even though it was clear he'd expected it, that admission seemed to rock Darren back on his heels. His eyes widened, and he looked away, a frown darkening his features. "Did you do this on purpose?"

Alex let out a sharp laugh. "You think I got pregnant on purpose?"

"I've heard of omegas doing things like this. Entrapping alphas—"

"You were the one coming on to me with all that 'You're my mate' and 'My wolf wants you' business. You got what you wanted. This is the result."

"And then you left!" Darren almost yelled. "You left me with nothing but a note. A note telling me that you couldn't stay in one place. You didn't even have the guts to tell me to my face."

"You're right. I didn't. And that was wrong. I acted like a selfish coward. But I told you that you deserved better than me!"

"You told me that *in your note*," Darren snarled. "I remember because I read it over and over again, trying to think of what I'd done wrong."

Alex closed his eyes and shook his head, feeling tired and sad and wishing he was anywhere else but here, having this fight.

"You didn't do anything wrong," Alex told him. "In fact, you did almost everything right. But I'm not what you think. I might be an omega, but I'm not some kind of kept pet. I have a job. A career."

"I never once thought of you as a pet. Never. Once."

"But you wanted me to stay here with you, even though my job as a photographer means I must travel. You expected me to give up everything. I know alphas. Don't try to deny it."

Darren slammed his fist down on the counter, making the plates rattle. "I wanted to help you! I wanted *you*!" He seemed to realize he was shouting and drew back. A strained smile crossed his face. He took a deep breath and let it out slowly. "Listen to me. You got me all tied up in knots." He glanced down at Alex's belly, and there was a flash of tenderness in his eyes. "Is it a boy or a girl?"

"Do you even care?"

Those words hurt Darren. Alex could see it the instant the words passed his lips. But it was too late to take them back now. More guilt hit him. He wasn't handling this well. Hurting Darren wasn't what he wanted. Not at all.

"Yes," Darren replied softly. "I do care."

Those simple words set off a burst of warmth in Alex's chest.

"It's a boy," he nearly whispered.

"A boy," Darren repeated and broke out in a beautiful smile.

Alex blinked back tears and turned away quickly, not wanting Darren to see him overwhelmed by his emotions.

Darren reached out a hand toward his belly but paused before touching him. "May I?"

Alex nodded. Darren put his big hand on Alex's belly. The baby immediately kicked and turned as if he recognized his father.

Darren laughed aloud at the feeling beneath his hand. He was watching Alex's belly, staring with an almost childlike wonder.

Darren withdrew his hand again. He looked Alex in the eye. "Thank you."

Again, Alex nodded, a lump in his throat making it hard to breathe. The man was thanking him? After all Alex had put him through?

Darren turned and walked to the refrigerator. "Are you hungry?"

"Seems like I'm always hungry these days."

"You should be. You're eating for two. I'll whip something up. You go ahead and sit on one of those stools and take it easy."

"You don't have to—"

"No. I do have to. But I need to have something for my hands to do so my mind can think. Steak and eggs okay? That's the extent of my culinary skills."

Alex felt his mouth water at the prospect. "That's fine." In fact, it was better than fine. It sounded great.

Darren took steaks out of the fridge and put out pans on the stovetop. "You look big. How close are you?"

"Eight months."

Darren froze for a moment, tensing up again. "And you didn't want to tell me until now?"

"I did want to tell you. Every day I wanted to tell you. But I was also afraid."

Darren turned to look him in the eye. "Afraid?

Why? I'd never hurt you."

"Because I had no idea how you were going to react. And…I ran out on you. So I knew you wouldn't want to see me on your doorstep again."

"You're wrong about that," Darren said. "Just like you're wrong about a lot of things."

Alex tried to think of an answer, but he didn't have a good one.

He stared at Darren's broad shoulders as the man turned back to the stove and busied himself over the pans and sizzling meat. He'd deserved that, he supposed. It was abundantly clear that things were far from settled. Darren hadn't slammed the door in his face. Darren hadn't thrown him out of his life. But that didn't mean things were okay between them.

Not by a long shot.

* * *

Darren's head was reeling. He hadn't believed his eyes when he'd opened the door to see Alex standing there. His heart felt as if it had crumpled itself up like a ball of aluminum foil.

His omega wolf had come home.

The man he'd never expected to see again. The man whose life he'd saved. The omega wolf now carrying his child. His mate had returned.

At first he was as angry about it as he was relieved, as thrilled as he was hurt. Alex never should've left in the first place. That was a given. But since he had, and since he'd come back…did that change things? Right now, he didn't know. His wolf was howling with joy and exulting in his mind, but that didn't mean things would work out.

And a kid… Darren was going to be a father. Something he knew for a fact that he wasn't ready for. Today his life was changing forever. The way it had changed forever when he'd rescued Alex from that burning building.

He flipped the steaks and added some onions and green peppers to the scrambled eggs he was cooking. The strangeness of having Alex sitting in his kitchen was churning up all kinds of emotions he'd long ago pushed out of his mind.

To think, this was his day off. He'd woken up, gone on his daily jog, lifted some weights, and gone on about his business as if it was a normal day. Never once had he expected to be ambushed and told he was going to be a father.

He could support a kid, no problem. Boy or girl, he didn't care. He wasn't one of those guys who had to have a son to carry on the family name or anything. He had a house, a steady job, so yeah, he could support a child. But Alex… There were so many things still up in the air.

He plated up the food and brought one of those plates to where Alex was sitting.

The omega looked good. Pregnancy agreed with him. His skin had a glow, and he'd filled out nicely when putting on weight for the baby. Of course, he looked rather awkward with that huge belly, but that was usual. Darren wasn't a fool, and he didn't have a death wish. He knew to keep his mouth shut about any comments on Alex's size.

Besides, part of him yearned to pull Alex into his arms and give him a long kiss, to claim those lips again. To let Alex and his wolf know that Darren was glad he was back. That Darren would set everything right again.

He took a stool opposite Alex, cut a piece of steak, and forked it into his mouth. "So you're back. What happens now? Are you going to leave the kid with me and then go off on your photography assignments again?"

The question made Alex flinch. His pretty eyes showed his hurt and uncertainty. Darren felt bad about calling out the omega, but he didn't want to spend all evening dancing around the truth either.

"No," Alex replied. "I'm not going to dump our kid on you and leave. I have a few work possibilities in the Chicago area."

"So you're staying in Chicago?" His heart began to beat faster. That opened all kinds of new and interesting possibilities.

"I'm going to try."

"But why? You wouldn't stay here before." That was still a wound in him. He thought the wound had healed over, but seeing Alex again had torn it right open again.

"The baby changes everything. He deserves to know you…if you're interested. If you're not…I'll go. But I had to take the chance. You deserved to know."

Darren nodded. "You were right to come. I won't lie. I was surprised as hell to see you. Right now, I don't know how I feel about it. This is a lot to take in all at once."

"I understand. You don't have to sugarcoat things either. I know we're on rocky ground."

They didn't talk much as they ate. Alex complimented him on the food. He smiled and shrugged. He wasn't a very accomplished cook, but he could fry up a few things decently. Soon he'd be bottle feeding an infant, then spooning baby food into his son's mouth, probably getting it everywhere. He'd have to master the art of macaroni and cheese for when his son was older.

This was all so unexpected and crazy. He felt so staggered that he knew he was numb with shock. The magnitude of all of this hadn't sunk in yet.

When they were done eating, he put the plates in the sink. "Do you have a name for the kid yet?"

"No, not yet. I was holding out until I talked to you."

Darren found himself touched by that. It did a little to soothe how angry and hurt he was that Alex had left him and kept this secret for so long. It certainly didn't make up for that, but it showed that at least Alex had started thinking of someone else besides himself and his career.

Maybe that was too harsh. Darren did understand that alphas could be overwhelming, wanting to protect and care for those they saw as part of their family and pack. He had intended to get Alex to stay here in Chicago with him almost from the moment he'd seen him. That relentless pursuit might have helped drive Alex away, smothered him, or made him feel trapped.

But Alex had come back. So that counted in his favor.

"Thank you for including me in choosing his

name," Darren told him. "I think we can probably come up with a good, strong name for a boy if we put our heads together."

He paused, wondering how much more he should say. He didn't want to drive the man off again. But he also didn't want to come across as too eager either. After all, Alex's leaving had ruffled more than his fur. If you had an unforgettable night fucking with your mate before your omega ran off into the wild the next morning, leaving nothing but a note, that wasn't something you could shake off right away. Even eight months later, it still hurt.

Alex carefully pushed himself off the stool. "I'd better go. I know this is a lot to take in." He paused, then looked in Darren's eyes. "I have a meeting with a new doctor in a couple days. You're welcome to come along."

"Do *you* want me to come?" he asked softly, his gaze never leaving Alex's face.

The little omega stood there boldly, without flinching. "I would like you to come."

"Then I'd be happy to."

"Do you…want to be with me when I give birth? You don't have to. I mean, it's not going to be a good time for anyone—"

Darren couldn't stand it anymore. He kicked logic out the window and gave himself over completely to instinct as he leaned in and captured the omega's soft lips with his own, silencing his words.

The kiss was tender, full of both promises and restraint. Alex tensed at first, surprised. Then he yielded, his eyes closing. His large belly pressed between them. Darren was mindful of it, but he had to admit that knowing his unborn child was inside the omega, safely right there between them, was a mind-blowing realization.

Slowly, he drew back. He hadn't intended to kiss Alex. Not after all that had happened. But when the omega had been going on, showing his doubts and fears, it had seemed the best way to reassure him. The best way to say so much without fumbling with awkward words.

His wolf certainly agreed. In fact, his wolf wanted more. Although he was going to have to wait on that front. He had the feeling that Alex wouldn't be in the mood to fool around for a while since fooling around with Darren had landed them both here in the first place.

"I do want to be with you when our child is born," Darren told him. "I'd be honored."

"Good," Alex said. "That's…good."

Alex still appeared shocked that Darren had kissed him. Shocked…and pleased.

Maybe he felt as conflicted about it as Darren did. Darren wasn't a man who usually spent a lot of time focused on his emotions, but this time he had given himself over to his instincts. Was he being too forgiving? Was he acting like a fool again? Maybe. But sometimes people needed a second chance. Wasn't that what Alex was asking for right now?

Between them, there was a moment of awkward, tense silence. There were so many things to say. He had never been good at saying them. Hell, give him a fire to fight or a burning building to charge into and he'd do it in a heartbeat. But all this emotional stuff was a jungle where you couldn't see six feet in front of you, full of vines to trip him up.

So he focused on solving problems instead of dwelling on the tangled knot of emotions that seeing his omega had stirred up in him again. "Do you have a place to stay?"

If he didn't, he was more than welcome to stay with Darren. He didn't want to throw that offer out there right away because he was afraid it would spook Alex. Right now, he didn't want to do anything to risk driving the omega away.

"I rented a furnished place a few miles away," Alex said softly. He sent a quick glance to Darren's eyes as if trying to read the emotions there. "It's just a small apartment, but it's enough for now."

Darren did his best to seem non-threatening and

to only be a supportive alpha. While his wolf definitely wanted Alex to move in here with him so he could keep an eye on the omega, he also realized that he had to take it slowly. Just seeing Alex again had eased some of the betrayed hurt and pain he'd felt ever since Alex had run out on him. No, it hadn't healed things completely, but just seeing him again, knowing he'd sought Darren out to include him in the birth of their child, helped a lot. He'd even held off picking a name so that Darren could participate.

That meant something, right?

But after his child was born, would he still be able to control the powerful instincts to provide for those he cared for? Did he want his child growing up in a one-room apartment? Did he have a choice if Alex kept custody and wasn't interested in accepting that he was Darren's mate?

Those were worrying thoughts. But there was no sense worrying about them now. One thing at a time.

"You might have a place already," he said. "But I want you to know you can always stay here." Some things needed to be said, and the omega needed to know that Darren wasn't going to turn him away.

Alex took a deep breath as if relieved. "Thank you. Would you like…?" He paused as if afraid to go on.

Darren frowned. "I don't bite, Alex. You know

that. Go ahead and ask."

"Would you like to come to my Lamaze classes? I signed up for them before I arrived…"

"If I'm going to be with you in the hospital, I guess I'd better know what's going to happen and help out if I can."

Now the relief was undeniably clear on Alex's face. "Okay. Okay, good. I'll give you my cell number and get yours, and I'll get you all the details."

"Sounds like a plan."

Alex hesitated. "Um. Like I said, I guess I'd better go… I still have a few errands to run."

"You have a car?"

"I do. I know, weird right? I figure if I'm going to be living in one place for a while, I should lease one. Otherwise hiring drivers is going to make me broke."

Darren hid his disappointment. He'd wanted to take Alex somewhere in his truck, to keep talking to him. He knew he should be angrier about all of this. He might even be justified in kicking the omega out of his house and telling him he never wanted to see him again.

But he simply wasn't that kind of person. Alex was back. His mate. The man whose life he'd saved. The man who made Darren's heart beat faster just seeing him, who made his chest tighten with the powerful feelings inside. His wolf felt a mix of pride that he'd gotten the omega pregnant and exultation that his mate had returned. Darren couldn't deny that.

"When will I see you again?"

"I have my new Lamaze class on Friday evening. If you'd like to come to it… I know it's short notice—"

"I would like to come," he said gravely.

He wanted to see Alex before that, perhaps take him to dinner or something, but he needed to fight his instincts and go slow. Alex had already done a lot to meet him halfway on this, coming here, inviting Darren to take part in the birth. He needed to respect that and let Alex take the lead for a while, no matter how difficult that was for the alpha in him to tolerate.

Alex's smile lit up his whole face. "I'll come pick you up."

Darren put a hand on the other man's shoulder, returning the smile. "No, let me drive. That way I can chauffeur you around and feel like I'm helping."

"I'd be all for that, except that I don't think I can get into your truck without a hydraulic lift."

Darren laughed. The man had a point. This was a whole new world for him and would take a new way of thinking. This was just the beginning too. After the baby came, he was going to have to deal with car seats and baby gates and childproofing and diaper disposal.

"You're right," Darren replied. "I'll give up the

truck, and we'll take your car."

Alex stared into his eyes, a faint blush on his cheeks. "You'd give up driving your truck just to come with me?"

"Of course I would. But if you want me to do the driving, I'd be happy to." He shrugged. "Whatever's best for you."

"You can drive my car. That way I don't have to deal with the steering wheel getting in the way of this basketball in my stomach."

"It's a deal."

He walked Alex out to his car. His wolf didn't want Alex to leave. The wolf was almost panicked about it, now that he'd suddenly reappeared in their life. He kept control like the alpha he was. He even managed to check the almost undeniable urge to kiss the other man, claiming his lips again. There would be time for that later.

Lots of time for it.

He stood there and watched Alex drive away. Then he went back inside, thinking about how everything had changed forever.

He felt like he'd been blindsided by a speeding truck. But at the same time, he felt more excited than ever for what was to come.

CHAPTER SEVEN

"Take your two cleansing breaths," the class instructor said. "Good. Now take a third breath and hold it. Let it out. New breath. We'll be doing this through the contraction, finishing with a cleansing breath."

Alex focused on his breathing. Darren was in front of him, looking into his eyes and counting with him. This was their third class together.

At first, he'd been sure the big firefighter would laugh at the Lamaze classes and wouldn't be willing to practice the techniques. But Darren had surprised him.

He'd thrown himself into it as if it was some kind of firefighter training. He was even more into it than Alex was. It was actually really endearing.

The two of them also had a bit of celebrity in the class. Alex was the only pregnant male, of course. The human couples were all fascinated by that. And yes, he'd gotten his fair share of jokes from the men. He'd rolled with those and teased back to show they didn't bother him. But Darren was also popular, catching more than a few admiring looks, especially from the class instructor.

Alex wasn't jealous. He thought it was amusing. Also, Darren seemed to be clueless about it. His attention was always focused on Alex like a laser. It was almost enough to give Alex a big head. One thing he really loved was getting massages from Darren. Or having Darren touch him. The alpha's touch soothed him and seemed to soothe the baby too.

The instructor began the question-and-answer segment she always kept at the end of class. Alex let his mind drift. He'd been doing this long enough to know the answers and had heard the usual questions from new couples many times before.

A few things were bothering him lately, although it was hard to put a finger on them. Sometimes he got the feeling that Darren was upset that Alex wasn't living in Darren's house but that the alpha was doing all he could to hide it. That made Alex a bit uneasy. He'd always been leery of the tendency of alphas to dominate. It was in their blood. Darren had already invited him to stay…but right now Alex thought they both needed some space. Especially after all that had happened, and all that had changed.

Alex wasn't dominate, of course. He was an omega wolf. The lowest rung on the pack ladder. But omega wolves were also rare and special, as the child inside him proved. That was a source of pride for him. So didn't intend to be anyone's submissive either. That was one of the biggest reasons he'd saved money for the furnished apartment he'd rented. Yes, part of him would've loved to have stayed with Darren. But part of him might've resented it too.

There was also the fact that he'd run off once already. That was probably making Darren nervous. Leaving had definitely been a mistake, especially the way he'd handled it. Sneaking off into the night like a thief. Darren had been angry and hurt, and Alex felt terrible about that.

The truth was, Alex was afraid.

He'd done all he could to keep that fear to himself, to hide it from Darren. He was afraid of the changes in his life after the child was born. He was afraid of Darren leaving him alone with the child…and he was afraid of

Darren keeping him as some kind of omega pet. He couldn't seem to find any middle ground.

Darren touched his shoulder, startling Alex out of his tense thoughts. "Class is over. You zoned out there during the Q and A."

He grinned self-consciously. "Whoops. I was lost in my thoughts." He glanced around quickly. "Did anyone notice?"

"No, your secret's safe with me. Anything good I need to know in those thoughts of yours?"

"No," Alex said, a bit too quickly.

Darren's eyes narrowed for a second, but he only nodded and let the matter go. Darren helped him back to his feet and put an arm around his shoulders. "You hungry?"

"These days I'm always hungry. You want me to cook something up?"

"I was thinking of heading to a place near the station. It's good. You'll like it. Local favorite."

"Sounds perfect."

They said goodbye to a few of the couples they'd come to know and left. Darren held the car door open for him as he climbed inside. Sometimes he found that amusing and sometimes he found it a little annoying, as if he couldn't open the door on his own. He was pregnant, not missing two hands. But he knew Darren's heart was in the right place. These days, he let Darren do the driving though. The alpha never once complained about driving the sedan Alex had leased instead of his big truck. He appreciated that. It meant a lot to Alex.

The place Darren took him to was a little sandwich shop on a quaint side street with lots of small, eclectic shops. Darren ordered a corned beef sandwich. Alex ordered a fried chicken sandwich loaded with lettuce, mayo, pickles, and fried in ham drippings and butter. His stomach was already rumbling, and his mouth was watering, just from the incredible scents.

They took their sandwiches and sat outside at a small iron table. It was early evening. The stars were starting to come out. The day had been warm, but now that the sun was down, it was starting to cool off nicely.

After he finished stuffing his big sandwich into his stomach, Alex leaned back in his chair with a deep sigh. He rested his hands on his belly. He could feel the baby kicking around, as he often did after a meal. The kid was probably going to be a big eater—especially given how big Darren was and how much he ate.

Darren grinned at him. "Is the little guy kicking again?"

"Like Bruce Lee." He reached out and took Darren's hand. "Here. Feel."

He guided Darren's hand to the place where their

baby was kicking.

Darren's grin went even wider, and he stared at Alex's belly in wonder. Just like he always did. This wasn't the first time he'd felt their baby kicking of course, but every single time seemed to amaze him. It was that childlike wonder that Alex sometimes saw in the alpha that really tugged at his heart. The man wasn't just a strong, brave firefighter who charged into burning buildings to save people. No, he also had the ability to take joy in the simplest things. There wasn't a cynical bone in the alpha's body, and Alex admired him for that.

Darren looked up and met his eyes. "I've been thinking about a name…"

"Yeah? Great! Let me hear it," Alex replied eagerly. He noticed that Darren seemed a little hesitant, and that wasn't like him at all.

"I'd like to name him Jonathan. If that's okay with you."

"That's a good, strong name." He paused, trying to read the other man's expression. He seemed so earnest about this name. "Does it have some special significance?"

"It was the name of a friend of mine when I was young. He lost his life in a fire. His father was a drunk. He passed out with a lit cigarette in his hand and caught the house on fire. It was a tragedy. Something I never forgot."

Alex's eyes immediately teared up, and his throat went tight with emotion. He was on an emotional hair trigger these days, but that story was so heartbreaking.

"Oh my God. I'm so sorry to hear that. Of course we can name him Jonathan. I think your friend would be honored."

Darren nodded. "I think he would be too."

"Was that…? Was that why you became a firefighter?"

"Yeah. Part of it anyway. A big part. I wanted to help people. I wanted to save lives. I graduated high school knowing exactly what I wanted to do with my life, and I've never had any regrets. Not for a second."

Alex looked away. He touched his belly defensively. "Not even now?"

"The only thing I'll regret is if my mate leaves me again."

That made Alex flinch. He threw a quick glance at Darren, seeing his fierce, almost challenging stare. "I…"

"You don't need to say anything right now. I'm not trying to put you on the spot or ruin our evening. I probably should've kept my mouth shut."

Alex shook his head. "No, you don't need to keep your mouth shut about that. I want to know how you feel. All I can say is that I came back…because of you.

Because I knew you'd be a great father."

"Will I?" Darren crossed his arms over his chest and leaned back. He looked off across the tall brick buildings that surrounded the sandwich shop.

"How can you say that?" He was shocked to hear any doubt in the alpha's voice. "You do a great job caring for me. You'll do a great job caring for our child."

"You make it sound like a sure thing. Kids are difficult. I know because I was a difficult kid."

"This is really bothering you, isn't it?" Alex asked softly, his eyes searching Darren's face. This shouldn't have surprised him. It was a common fear. Heck, he felt it himself, doubting whether he'd be a good parent to the new life who depended on him. But Darren always seemed so confident. So…alpha.

"Yeah, it bothers me. This isn't something you can train for. What if I'm bad at it?"

Alex reached out and gave his hand a squeeze. "Every parent is in the same place."

"You're right, but I don't have to like it."

"No, I guess you don't," Alex replied, laughing gently. "But you need to believe me when I say you'll be a great father. Everything I know about you makes me believe that with all my heart."

Darren seemed pleased by his words. Alex suddenly felt powerful being the one to reassure him for once. It made him feel like they were more of a team, a couple, instead of it just being him relying on the alpha for everything.

"So…after the baby is born," Darren said. His eyes were intense. "What happens then?"

Alex hesitated, his stomach tightening with sudden concern. "What do you mean?"

"I mean, do you go off disappearing again? Do you mean to take our kid with you? Or are you going to leave him with me? Maybe it's time we finally talk about that."

Panic burst in his mind. This wasn't a conversation he wanted to have now or here. Mostly because he hadn't decided, and so much depended on what Darren wanted. "I…don't think I'm ready to make that decision."

"What do you mean you're not ready to make that decision? The baby's due in two weeks! Please tell me you've at least thought about it."

Tension began to churn in Alex's gut. He deliberately hadn't thought about it. Right now, he was only focused on giving birth to a healthy child. Everything else in the future was a nightmare of stress and uncertainty. Did he give up his life of travel forever, his career forever because he had a child? Did he rely on Darren to take care of him and completely become an omega? And what was best for little Jonathan? Having two parents would be best, of course, but maybe Alex wasn't ready to give up everything under pressure from Darren.

Or maybe he was.

He decided he had to come back strong against the pressure as Darren confronted him. That was the only thing that Darren would understand. Coming back strong and telling the truth.

"I haven't thought about it because I've been focused on giving birth to our child. Everything beyond my due date is a big, shadowy question. But it's not a question I need to have answered right now, so it can wait. I have a place for him to stay and a car I can drive, so I'm not panicking about that. What I'm panicking about is childbirth and making sure everything goes well. I know you want a different answer, but that's what I'm thinking about right now."

Darren closed his eyes and nodded as if mulling over Alex's words. "You're right. That's what you should be focused on. I was out of line." He toyed with the red plastic basket his sandwich had been served in. "I keep thinking about it because I want to plan for the future. I guess I just assumed that we would get through this and everything would be okay."

"The same way I assume that you're going to be a

great father?" Alex asked gently, raising an eyebrow.

"Yeah. The same way, I guess." His stare was intense and focused. "I promise you, we'll both get through this. I'll be right beside you every step of the way. Until our baby is born, and after, if that's what you want." He leaned forward, pinning Alex with his gaze. "Because it's what I want."

"I know." Warmth spread through him, pushing away the fear and worry.

Darren got out of his chair and moved around the table to squat down beside Alex, resting a hand on his thigh. His expression was very serious.

"You have faith in me being a good father," he said. "Hearing that from your lips has helped me believe it. I'm still worried, but maybe that worry will keep me on my toes. Now have faith in me being there for you, Alex. Being there for you and for Jonathan. I will not let you down. You are my mate."

Alex took a deep, shuddering breath. He hadn't even decided on what he wanted to say in reply before Darren reached out and cupped his cheek and drew him into a kiss.

The kiss was amazing, both tender and loving and still with an underlying flash of heat and passion. It made him yearn to be in Darren's arms, safe and warm and wanted. It made him want to kiss the alpha all over his body. It made him want Darren inside him again, driving them both wild with pleasure.

Darren ended the kiss. As he drew back, he traced a gentle finger along Alex's jawline, his eyes soft with love.

Inside Alex, his wolf was howling with pleasure at the alpha's words and his kiss. His heart was soaring too. What more did he need to hear? Why couldn't he simply accept this blessing in his life?

Things had changed. He needed to change too. He was strong enough to do it. With Darren at his side, he was even stronger.

"I know you won't let me down," Alex said. "And thank you. Thank you for letting me back into your life. You didn't have to do that."

"Of course I did," Darren replied simply. "What kind of man would I be if I didn't?"

Alex didn't say anything. Darren was too good a man. Alex was a fool to be worried about all the things that had been troubling him. Why was he looking for trouble?

He needed to stop being so selfish and be there for Darren too. He needed to let him know that he was going to be a good father. He needed to show Darren that he realized the firefighter was one in a million.

But first he had to get through the rest of this

pregnancy. Once that was behind him, he could finally find the courage to tell Darren that he was falling in love with him. All that mate stuff from the wolves was fine, but day by day, action by action, Darren was winning his heart.

He only hoped he proved worthy of that kind of dedication.

CHAPTER EIGHT

Alex was due any day now. The last month had passed in a haze, seeming to blur past him. Darren had attended every Lamaze class. The alpha had thrown himself into learning all he could, whether that was attending classes or reading books. It was clear he wanted to be the best partner possible.

Thinking about it made Alex's throat tight and made him feel like crying, as silly as that was. Darren was a good man. He was always thinking about the baby. True, he might be a bit controlling, but that was the alpha side of him coming out. Alex understood it. He didn't always like it, but he had his own shortcomings. It was clear that Darren was doing his best to rein in that part of him in for Alex's sake.

Darren had taken him out to dinner several times to good local places around the city. He'd taken Alex to see an action movie, then fretted that the explosions would be too loud for the baby. Even though they'd shared nothing more than kisses because Alex simply didn't feel attractive or comfortable enough for sex right now, the alpha's attraction was clear and never wavered. They were feelings that Alex shared.

These days they were both on edge, waiting for the baby to come. Alex was more than ready to stop feeling like a very large mammal. Or at least feeling like a mammal who carried around a bowling ball in his abdomen.

He was frightened about what was to come and doing his best not to show it. But as much as he tried to hide it, it seemed like Darren could sense it. He was especially caring and kind and supportive.

Alex didn't know what he'd do without his mate there by his side.

His due date was officially still two days away, but he'd woken up feeling restless this morning. He'd cleaned his small apartment rigorously. Then he'd driven to Darren's house and let himself in with the key Darren had given him. He'd gone on to clean Darren's place as well from top to bottom. Strangely, he found all this cleaning to be soothing.

But damn, he wanted to have this baby. Not only was he eager to meet the new life inside him, he was done with all the pregnancy-brain forgetfulness. He was tired of odd cravings for peanut butter cookies and sourdough bread. He was tired of feeling tired. Except now he wasn't feeling tired at all. He felt like he wanted to clean the entire world, even the water-spotted windows, so the baby would be impressed when it came out.

He was carrying his cell phone in his pocket so it would always be within reach. As he finished loading Darren's dishwasher, he got a call from Darren.

"How are you doing?" Darren asked right away. The usual concern was in his voice. Sometimes Alex felt like the alpha believed he was made out of glass and would break at any moment. But other times the man's concern touched him. This was one of those times when it touched his heart.

"I'm okay. Just cleaning a little."

"Shouldn't you be lying down, taking it easy?"

Alex snorted. "No. I'm not on bed rest, and my leg isn't broken. This keeps my mind occupied."

Darren was quiet for a moment. "I guess that

makes sense. Are you home?"

"I'm at your place."

Another moment of silence. Then Darren's voice came back over the phone sounding confused. "You're cleaning *my* house?"

"I already cleaned my apartment. I needed something else to clean."

"I'm not even going to ask."

"That's probably wise." Sometimes it was hard to remain patient with people who weren't pregnant. Especially men, who were generally clueless. Talking with women at the classes was great, but he wished he knew a few omega wolves to vent with. Sometimes he felt a little isolated…

No, he wasn't going to let himself feel down or irritated right now. He was too busy feeling restless. He chatted a bit with Darren, who was taking lunch down at the station, and then let him go back to work. Thinking of lunch made him hungry, so he headed to the fridge and made himself a big sandwich with roast beef and spicy peppers and hot sauce. It tasted…odd…but spicy, and that seemed to make him feel a little steadier.

After that, he paced Darren's house, hauling himself from room to room and staring out the windows at the street or the yard. He wasn't looking for anything in particular, but his brain seemed stuck in neutral.

Twenty minutes later, the first contraction hit. Well, the first of the day. He'd had some false labor two days ago, but they hadn't gone to the hospital before the contractions had faded.

This one felt sharp, powerful.

He went to the couch and sat down. He practiced his breathing techniques while timing the contractions.

They were strong contractions, lasting about a minute. And they were coming about four minutes apart. His heart began to pound faster. That was within the range where they recommended you head to the hospital.

He snatched up his phone and speed dialed Darren. Relief shot through him when Darren answered on the second ring.

"I'm in labor," Alex said breathlessly, jumping right into it. He didn't have time for small talk. "Can you take me the hospital?"

"I'm on my way," Darren said. He didn't sound worried or shaken. He sounded driven, a man on a mission. "I have a go bag in the closet near the foyer. Grab it and wait for me. And Alex?"

"Yes?"

"Don't worry. You're going to be fine. I'll be right there by your side the whole time."

"I know..." Alex whispered. He could hear

Darren hurrying through the fire station. He wanted to see the man so badly now. He needed him by his side, holding his hand. He didn't care if anyone laughed at him. He wanted his mate with him now.

"Our baby is coming," Darren continued. "We're going to meet him today."

Alex wiped away hot tears that streamed down his face. "You're right. I'm so ready to meet him."

"I'm going to hang up now, Alex," Darren informed him. "But rest assured I'm on my way to you right now. You're still at my place?"

"Yeah, still there. Don't drive too fast. Both of us don't need to end up in the hospital."

"Good point. Now sit down if you're not sitting already and practice your breathing. I'll be there as soon as I can."

Darren disconnected. Alex leaned back against the couch. He waited for the next contraction to hit, practicing everything he'd learned in class. He couldn't lie though. Part of him was terrified of what was coming. Part of him was excited to have it over with and hold his child in his arms.

As he waited, time felt slower than molasses. It seemed like minutes stretched out into hours. It was a weird, painful, distracting feeling having his muscles harden and tighten almost as if he was experiencing terrible cramps. Breathing through them helped. It made him feel as if he still had control of things.

Darren's go bag sat at his feet, ready for him to take along to the hospital. The bag was packed with socks, slippers, lotion, sports drinks, changes of clothing, bendy straws, and toiletries. Then there were blankets and hats for the baby. Tiny diapers. Darren had seemed to think of everything.

Another strong contraction hit him hard when Darren burst through the door. His expression was serious, his eyes focused. He was all business. In control and getting things done.

"How are you doing?" he asked as he hurried across the room. He went down to one knee and took Alex's hand in both of his own.

"I'm fine." He stopped, laughed and shook his head. "That's not true. I'm terrified. I don't know if I'm ready for this."

Darren squeezed his hand. "You are ready for this, Alex. I know how strong you are. Like I said, I'll be right here with you the entire time."

Alex smiled. Darren's words made him feel better. "I wouldn't have it any other way. Now what do you say we get going? I don't want to have this baby while trapped in rush-hour traffic."

"Good point." Darren grabbed the go bag and

helped Alex to his feet. Together, they headed down to Alex's car. Halfway there, Alex had to stop and breathe through another contraction. Darren rubbed his shoulders and murmured encouragement to him until the contractions faded.

"Just you wait," Alex said, his voice unsteady. "After this gets worse, I get to yell at you for doing this to me."

Darren chuckled. "I'll take any blame you want. Right now, you're the most beautiful thing in the world, and I'll fight anyone who says differently."

Alex smiled. Those words were ones he wanted to remember when things got sweaty and painful during this birth.

When he stepped outside, he was shocked to see a fire truck sitting parked at the curb. There were a bunch of firefighters standing around it. They cheered as soon as they saw him.

He was blushing furiously as he glanced at Darren. "You brought the entire fire station along with you?"

Darren grinned and winked. "Not the entire station. Just a few of the boys. And how else could I give you an emergency escort to the hospital?"

His eyes widened. "Is that even legal?"

"Gray area. If a call comes in, they'll need to leave.

But just cross your fingers that we don't get a call and we can get to the hospital in style."

"If you say so—" His words were cut off by a gasp as another contraction hit him.

Darren hustled him to Alex's car and helped him inside. He tossed the go bag in the back. Then he waved to his firefighter buddies, and they all pulled away. The fire truck turned on its siren as it started down the road. Even though they never once exceeded the speed limit, cruising through red lights was a definite perk and time saver.

It looked like having an alpha wolf firefighter for a mate had a few unexpected perks.

He realized he was tensed up, breathing fast, worried about what was to come. He began to do his breathing exercises, praying they would work as well as they claimed in the child-birthing classes. After a moment, Darren reached over, took his hand and squeezed it.

Alex squeezed back, taking all the comfort he could get. But with Darren at his side, he thought he just might get through this.

* * *

This had been one of the hardest things Darren had ever done...and he wasn't even the one giving birth.

His wolf had been going crazy, seeing his mate in pain. He relentlessly tried to keep focused on being there for Alex, on encouraging and supporting him no matter what. He might technically be a bit of a third wheel right now, but they were partners in this. They were mates. And his job was to help Alex with breathing through the contractions, giving him encouragement, wiping his sweaty brow, giving him slivers of ice or sips from energy drinks whenever he needed it.

Now it was finally over after eight hours of labor. Alex had given birth to a beautiful, healthy baby boy.

When the doctor finally settled a squalling, tiny baby in Alex's arms, Darren knew he had never seen anything so beautiful and precious. Watching Alex talk to the gorgeous life they'd made together made his heart fill with happiness. He was proud. He was damn proud of Alex, and he was proud of his little son.

The nurse took their child to put on an ID band, weighed him and took measurements, then his footprint.

After that, Darren had almost been nervous about taking the baby in his arms for the first time. A big, strong firefighter like him afraid? It was crazy, but as eager as he was, he also felt the huge weight of responsibility on his shoulders. He needed to do all he could for their child. He would protect it and love it always.

When the nurse put his baby boy in his arms, he cradled little Jonathan as if he were made of ice. His son was so tiny and perfect. Darren couldn't help the huge grin on his face as he stared down into Jonathan's small, sleeping face. He realized with a bit of shock that happy tears were running down his cheeks.

"You two are perfect for each other," Alex said from the hospital bed. His face was pale. He looked utterly exhausted. All the same, he gave Darren a tired, happy smile. "I'm the luckiest wolf in the world."

Darren slowly rocked his little child in his arms. He grinned at Alex. "No, I'm going to have to disagree with you, my friend. Right now, *I'm* the luckiest wolf in the world. But you're the real hero. You were brilliant. Everything about you was perfect."

Alex's tired smile widened a little. "Now you're just buttering me up. I feel like I ran two marathons back to back before a steamroller ran me over and a building fell on me."

"That's about how I imagined it feeling," Darren said with a laugh. Little Jonathan stirred in his arms. He made gentle shushing noises and rocked from side to side to soothe his baby. God, this felt amazing. He might look like a big fool, standing there with tears on his cheeks, cooing to his baby, but he didn't give a damn. This was a perfect moment.

He glanced at Alex and saw the man watching him with such a look of love on his face that Darren's heart felt as if it might melt.

The nurse came and took the baby for the nursery, to clean him and give an exam, promising to bring Jonathan back as soon as they were done. He reluctantly handed over his child. He knew it was necessary, but right now all he wanted to do was be here with Alex and hold their son. He wanted to revel in this miracle forever.

The room cleared out. He went to take the chair next to Alex. He reached out and took the other man's hand in his own, gently stroking it.

"You can't deny it now," Alex said in a tired voice. "I saw you with our son. I saw that look on your face. You love him."

"More than anything in the world." His mouth actually ached from grinning so hard. "Thank you, Alex. Thank you for giving me this…" He shook his head, his throat tight with emotion. He forced himself to continue. "For giving me this wonderful, amazing, priceless gift."

Alex blinked back tears, swallowing hard. "Thank you for being here with me," he whispered back.

"I wouldn't be anywhere else in the world."

Alex smiled and leaned his head back against the

pillow. He closed his eyes. Darren waited with him, listening to the sounds of the hospital and the nurses talking softly at their station.

When he glanced at Alex after a few minutes, he realized Alex was fast asleep. There were lines of strain on his face, his hair was sweaty, his skin a little pale, but he had never looked more beautiful to Darren. He was so proud of his omega. His little mate was a hero in his book.

He looked forward to being with Alex and Jonathan for as long as he could imagine.

* * *

It was two days later when the hospital finally released Alex and little Jonathan with a clean bill of health. Darren had spent much of the time since Jonathan was born building cribs and assembling electric swing sets, bouncers, and bassinets. He loved doing it, even if things like the playpen or all the baby-proofing wouldn't really be useful for a while. It made him feel like he was building a home, providing for the people who relied on him. It made him feel like he was making the world a better place. That might sound silly, so he kept it to himself, but he couldn't deny the truth of it either.

"How are you feeling?" he asked Alex as he pushed him through the hospital in a wheelchair. The hospital was big on moving people around in wheelchairs, but he was happy to steer Alex through the mazes of floors and elevators while Alex carried Jonathan in his arms.

"Happy," Alex answered, staring down into Jonathan's sleeping face. "Ready to go home."

"I hear you."

He didn't say what was really on his mind. He wanted Alex to move in with him. He just needed to find the right time to bring it up. And he needed to be careful. If he came on too aggressively, he might only succeed in driving Alex away. That was the last thing in the world he wanted.

They were soon all signed out. He was going to leave Alex here with Jonathan in the hospital's main lobby and bring Alex's leased sedan into the loading zone so Alex didn't have to walk far. He'd installed the car seat and checked it three times. He was a firefighter—he actually showed people how to install their car seats all the time—but still, he kept double-checking his work. He wouldn't compromise when the safety of his boy was at stake.

He parked the wheelchair near one of the big windows looking out at the courtyard fountain in front of the hospital. The bright, late afternoon sunlight made the clouds seem vibrantly white. The leaves of the small trees in planters trembled in the wind.

Darren frowned, hoping the wind wouldn't be too chilly. It looked warm enough out, but maybe he should get Alex another blanket. Would a thermal blanket be too much?

On second thought, he was being overprotective. As an alpha, he was going to have to find a balance with those powerful urges. Otherwise he might end up driving Alex away again.

But eventually they were going to have to sit down and have a long talk. Because he couldn't go through life constantly walking on eggshells hoping that Alex wouldn't vanish again. They needed to come to an agreement. A compromise if necessary. That wasn't too much to ask. He might be an alpha, but Alex and Jonathan were too important to him to risk ever losing.

"Wait here," he told Alex. "I'll get the car and bring it closer to the doors so you don't have far to walk."

Alex grinned. "Wow. Feels like I'm a VIP."

"Yeah, well, you *are* a VIP in my book." He chuckled and checked on Jonathan quickly. "Both of you are."

With that, he went to fetch the car. He hurried through the parking lot until he found the sedan. And he couldn't help it. He checked the car seat restraints one last time.

A few minutes later, he parked in the hospital's loading zone outside the main entrance. Then he brought in the detachable car seat/infant carrier. Together, they got Jonathan into the restraints, and Jonathan helped by sleeping peacefully through the whole thing. Then they made sure the baby's hat was on right and that he was snug in his blankets.

Darren held the carrier in one hand and put his arm around Alex's shoulders. Alex slipped his arm around his waist and let Darren support some of his weight.

They went slowly to the car. Darren clicked the infant carrier into the car seat base…and checked all the straps again. He was turning into an obsessive-compulsive, but as a firefighter and first responder, he'd seen too many accidents not to be a bit overprotective, maybe even a Nervous Nelly.

Alex chuckled. "You look like you've done that before."

"I'm a professional," Darren shot back with a grin. "Now for you."

He opened the door with a sweeping bow as if he were some kind of chauffeur or doorman. A bit of color came to Alex's cheeks as he smiled. He slowly eased himself down into the car with a wince. Darren knew he was on some mild pain medication and was still aching from the birth.

After Alex was safely clicked in, Darren hurried around to the driver side, started the car, and pulled away. He was excited and eager to get Alex and Jonathan home, but he drove very defensively.

So defensively that even Alex noticed.

"I'm not going to say you're driving like an old lady," Alex told him, "but I think my grandma just lapped us…on her personal mobility device."

"Ha. Ha. Very funny. This is defensive driving at its finest. I have very important cargo on board, I'll have you know."

"You're right. And I love you for it. But we're not nitroglycerine. You can go the speed limit."

Darren felt a thrill shoot through him—and a wave of shock—at what his mate had just said. Had Alex just used the "love" word? It had clearly been an off-the-cuff comment, but still, he liked the sound of that word coming out of his mate's mouth.

He was going to go for it. He was going to ask Alex to move in with him. The three of them could be a family. This seemed like the perfect moment.

Right now, he was driving into the neighborhood where Alex was renting the apartment. Darren had taken some leave from the station to be with Alex and help him out. He was going to be sleeping on the couch but ready to help care for their baby. Even though he'd agreed to that, he still wanted so much more. Alex's apartment was small, and the neighborhood was noisy. Why should Alex have to pay rent on this place, especially when Darren had more than enough room for all three of them?

Besides, he wanted his mate and his child in his life every minute he could have them. He wanted them close. He wanted all three of them sharing a roof together.

"Listen, Alex," he started. "I'm just going to come out and say this. Why don't you move in with me? That way I can be there for you and Jonathan all the time."

Alex looked at him quickly, then looked back out the window, a slight frown on his face.

He didn't answer right away, which made Darren nervous. Darren wasn't a man who got nervous often, but he *really* wanted this. Maybe he wanted it far more than Alex wanted it.

"I want this Alex," he continued. He paused, trying to gather his thoughts. He wasn't used to showing a lot of emotion either, but maybe he needed to right now. Maybe he needed to show what was in his heart in order to convince Alex of how he felt. "Give it a chance. Please. Let me show you I can be a good mate."

Alex took a deep, shuddering breath. "I know you can be a good mate. I'm not blind or stupid. You're a good man, Darren. You've done so much to care for me since I came back. You don't need to prove yourself to me."

"Don't I though?" he asked sharply but still keeping his voice down so he didn't wake the baby. "Then why do you fight so hard to keep distance between us sometimes?"

As he spoke, they reached Alex's apartment complex. He pulled into Alex's spot and parked, then turned his full attention to Alex.

"Why?" Alex repeated. "Because I'm afraid. Everything in my life has changed since I met you…"

"Yeah, it has. Especially considering that I saved your life and then got you pregnant." He hoped being blunt would help them push past this last barrier. "I've been holding myself back because I'm afraid you're going to run again—"

"No," Alex interrupted. "I'm not going to do that again. I promise you. That was a mistake."

Darren nodded, relief sweeping through him. That

was a good start.

"All right. Good. But I don't want you to be afraid of me, Alex. What can I do to make you feel safe?"

Alex barked a laugh. "Safe? I feel safer in your arms than with anyone else in the world. That's why I'm afraid. Because the omega part of me wants to settle down in those big, strong arms of yours and never leave. The omega wolf would give up every part of me to be with you. But what kind of life is that? Is that even love?"

"It's not love," Darren said, meeting Alex's eyes. "That's instinct. But you need to trust your heart. I'm a simple man, but I know my heart. My heart wants you in my life. Since you came back, I've never been happier. That's the truth."

"Same with me," Alex whispered, blinking back tears. One escaped and ran down his cheek.

Smiling a little, Darren reached out and tenderly wiped the tear away. God, he loved this little wolf. He only wanted to make him happy. Because Alex had made him so very happy, bringing Jonathan into his life.

Darren had feared he wouldn't be a good father. Those fears hadn't gone away completely, but the moment he'd held his son he'd known he could do this. He could love this child with all his heart. He would teach him to be a good, honorable man.

He could do it, and he *would* do it.

"Then what do you say? Move in with me. This weekend. I don't want to be away from you."

He decided to press his luck and leaned forward for a kiss. To his delight, Alex tilted his head and closed his eyes, allowing Darren to kiss him.

Alex's lips were soft and warm. His mate's scent filled him. Touching him, Darren knew he'd asked for the right thing.

They belonged together.

Darren drew back slightly but stayed close, looking into Alex's eyes. "Make me a happy man. I know I can make the both of you feel happy and loved. You don't even have to sleep in my bed if you don't want to. If it's too soon. It's all your call, my little wolf."

"Are you kidding?" Alex said, a smile twitching on his lips. "Of course I'll share your bed. I wouldn't give that up…although you'll have to wait a few more weeks for me to fully recover."

"Of course," Darren replied quickly. "I wouldn't dream of hurting you."

"I know you wouldn't. Yes. Yes, I'll move in with you. I think…I think it's time I put my money where my mouth is and really start believing in us."

Darren kissed him again, putting all his love, all his passion into the kiss. It was a glorious kiss…but then little Jonathan woke up and began his cute little "waah" hungry cry.

They both turned to look in the back of the sedan to the rear-facing car seat. Alex grinned. "Someone's hungry. Come on. Let's get him inside, and all three of us can have a bite to eat."

"Sounds like heaven," Darren said and meant every word.

CHAPTER NINE

It had been three weeks since Alex had moved into Darren's house. It had been a perfect, sleepless blur of a time. The baby was sleeping a little longer now between feedings. Not all night, not even close, but at least Alex and Darren could get a few consecutive hours of sleep.

But Alex wasn't sleeping right now. He was standing in the kitchen in a daze. The clock on the oven said two-thirty a.m. He blinked blearily at the baby formula he was carefully warming.

Meanwhile, Darren was walking around the

kitchen island holding a crying Jonathan. The alpha was bouncing him gently and singing Johnny Cash songs to him. Jonathan wouldn't be soothed though. His "hungry" cry echoed through the kitchen.

"Maybe he doesn't like Johnny Cash," Alex murmured as he checked the formula temperature for what felt like the tenth time.

"That's blasphemy," Darren said, still staring down into Jonathan's tiny face, all red and pinched up from crying. "Don't listen to your other dad, little guy. He's clearly sleep deprived."

"You and me both."

He had no idea how Darren could still head off to the station to fight fires and be a first responder with this little sleep. All day long, Alex felt fuzzy-headed and exhausted. Jonathan was a wonder, a true blessing in his life, but sometimes Alex missed sleep. Someday, when Jonathan was finally sleeping through the night, Alex was going to sleep for six days straight. He was going to be in a voluntary coma. That sounded like heaven right now.

Darren began to sing again, rocking Jonathan gently. Now he was singing "Somewhere Over the Rainbow." He actually had a good, strong singing voice. It was a deep baritone, and he could stay in key most of the time too. Alex closed his eyes and just listened.

His mate's voice was so soothing he almost forgot what he was doing. Of course, hungry little Jonathan wouldn't allow that. The kid had a set of lungs on him. Maybe he'd turn out to be an opera singer. Right now, as exhausted as Alex felt, he was hoping the kid grew up to be a mime. Or a monk taking a vow of silence.

Finally, the formula was the right temperature. He tested it on his inner wrist one last time. Perfect. "All right. Let me have that wailing bundle of joy so I can feed him."

Darren grinned at him and reached out for the bottle. "Here, let me feed him. You go back to bed. You look like you've been run over by a garbage truck."

Alex snorted and raised one eyebrow. "And that's how you talk to your mate who brought your child into the world?" He yawned. "I'm going to have to remember to be upset about this in the morning."

Darren took the bottle and began to feed Jonathan. The baby took the bottle eagerly, blinking and looking up at Darren as he ate. It was always a scene that touched Alex's heart, seeing the two of them together. The look of love in Darren's eyes as he gazed down at his son was enough to melt Alex's heart.

This was too good to be true. As he watched the two of them, it really began to sink in how much things had changed. He'd been a bit of an emotional wreck during his pregnancy, crying over happy movies and even tearing up over kids in diaper commercials.

But since he'd given birth, there had been a strange mix of the highest joy and...fear. Worry. A feeling of claustrophobia. It wasn't simply being tied to a child. It wasn't Darren's fault. It certainly wasn't the fault of their beautiful miracle of a baby. But he was feeling restless and distracted...almost anxious. He wasn't even sure why.

Was he crazy? Was his head broken in some way? Should he talk to someone? He didn't feel like he could talk to Darren about it. He wanted Darren to respect him, to love him. He didn't want to seem weak for his mate. Everyone knew omegas were weak. Everyone expected it. Alex had been dealing with that his entire life, and he hated it.

But especially this last week, he'd been feeling anxious. Maybe it was the lack of sleep. Maybe it was all the changes. Secretly, he'd searched the Internet, trying to understand the anxiety, the restlessness that hid beneath his smiles. It wasn't postpartum depression. He was pretty sure of that. He didn't feel hopeless or sad really. He adored his baby. He had a wonderful man who was amazing to him and to their child.

Maybe that was it. His life had always been a struggle. He'd always been on the move, never staying in one country for long. Was he feeling tied down? Stuck with no options? And how selfish was that? He hated himself for feeling that way. Men and women would kill to have what he had right now. All his needs provided for, a loving mate, a healthy, happy baby. Well, happy when he wasn't hungry that was.

He was an idiot. He wasn't worthy of Darren. What did he really bring to this relationship? He was basically mooching off Darren's kindness. They weren't even married. How long would it be before Darren grew tired of him and kicked him out? Maybe even filed for custody of Jonathan—

No, what the hell was wrong with him? He closed his eyes and took a deep breath, fighting back the rising panic inside him.

Darren didn't seem to realize anything was wrong. He was so focused on Jonathan. He was still rocking the child gently, helping hold the bottle for his son. The sight was so simple and yet so beautiful that Alex had to bite his lip and blink back tears. His emotions were out of control. He felt exhausted, worthless, trapped. In his mind, he knew that only the first of those three things held any merit. All the same, he couldn't seem to shake those feelings, no matter how much he knew them to be foolish.

"I think I'll take you up on that offer to head to

bed," he said quietly. "I'm so tired, I can't even see straight."

Darren glanced at him. Now he seemed to sense something was wrong. His brow furrowed. "You do look really exhausted. You feeling okay?"

Alex waved a hand to shush away his mate's concern. "Of course. Just tired. Maybe he'll sleep the rest of the night. Wouldn't that be a miracle?"

"Everything about him is a miracle," Darren said. He met Alex's eyes. "And you are too."

"Thank you." He padded over on bare feet to Darren. The big man leaned down to kiss him gently on the lips. After the kiss, Alex looked down at Jonathan who was staring at him with big blue eyes. "You be good for your dad, you hear me, little man?"

Jonathan only blinked at him, greedily sucking from the bottle.

Alex leaned in and kissed his baby, then made his way back to the bedroom. He collapsed into bed. But now he was so tired he couldn't sleep. He lay there, staring at the ceiling, wondering what the hell was wrong with him.

He might have given up his life of travel, of taking photos around the world as a freelancer, but now he had so much more. He had a place to stay. He had a beautiful child. He had a man who loved him. So why did he feel like he was losing control of his future?

Or that he already had lost control.

Why was he being stupid and selfish? He couldn't even talk to someone else about it because they would tell him exactly that. That he was being stupid and selfish and self-absorbed.

They wouldn't be wrong, either.

Tears began to run down his cheeks as he lay there in the dark. After a little while, Darren came in with Jonathan and carefully placed him in the bassinet. Jonathan stirred a little, and Darren quickly pushed the button that started to play soothing classical music pieces.

Jonathan settled down, and Alex heard Darren's grateful exhale of breath. It only made him love the man all the more. And that made Alex feel even worse for all the knots of emotion that were tightening inside him.

He had his eyes closed, but he could feel Darren turn his way, looking at him. He pretended to be asleep, praying the man wouldn't see the glitter of tears on his cheeks in the darkness.

After a moment, Darren climbed into bed beside him. He put his strong, warm arm around Alex.

Finally, Alex was able to fall asleep.

* * *

The next morning, Alex was sitting with Darren at the breakfast nook in the kitchen. Jonathan was secure in his bouncer, sleeping away with a bit of drool on those big baby lips.

Darren was shoveling down the pancakes and bacon Alex had cooked for him. Alex was only nursing a cup of coffee. He didn't have much appetite in the mornings anymore. He didn't know why. He'd always loved breakfast before. Maybe it was just another in a long line of changes in his life.

He held the coffee cup in both hands, reveling in the warmth seeping through the ceramic and into his joints. Strangely, he had the desire to shift into his wolf and go running through the trees with Darren, maybe at Starved Rock State Park or the Des Plaines river trails. He'd looked them up online, and they sounded perfect. Especially because he realized they had never even run together as wolves since they'd met.

Tears suddenly flooded his eyes. He tried to blink them away and hide them from Darren, but a sob escaped his lips.

Darren stopped eating and looked up.

"What's wrong?" Darren demanded, concern flashing in his eyes.

"Nothing..."

"Don't tell me that. Something's wrong. Tell me."

There was alpha command in his tone. Alex's omega wolf whined in his head, wanting to give in and obey. Alex gritted his teeth and pushed the wolf deeper into his mind where it couldn't interfere. He didn't need its primal instincts making this even harder.

"We haven't even shifted together," he said. "Our wolves have never been together."

Darren blinked at him. He seemed to be caught off guard by Alex's tears and the pain in his voice.

"Well..." Darren said carefully, eyeing Alex as if he might be a bit off his rocker, which only made him feel worse. It made him feel foolish and emotional and out of sorts. "We didn't have a chance when we first met." He paused, as if unsure if he wanted to bring up the fact that Alex had run off on him. But then he pressed on. "After that, you were pregnant, which meant no shifting." He glanced over at Jonathan, sleeping in the infant bouncer. "And then you gave birth, and we've been taking care of a newborn infant. So of course we haven't run together. That doesn't mean we will never get the chance."

"I'm a terrible mate," Alex blurted out. "What do you even see in me?" He looked away, hot tears burning on his cheeks. "I don't even have a steady job anymore. I'm just… I don't know how much of this…"

He bit his tongue to stop from going on. He didn't want to hurt Darren's feelings. But right now, even the man's calm explanations irritated him. They made him feel like a child.

Frowning, Darren set down his fork and reached across the table to take his hand. "Listen to me, Alex. Things won't be like this forever. We'll do all the things as a couple that we missed out on. I promise you. I will take care of you both."

He pulled his hand away and stood on shaky legs. "Maybe that's the problem. Maybe I don't want to be cared for as if I was some kind of dependent. Maybe I want to bring just as much worth to this relationship as you bring."

His voice had grown a little too loud. The baby stirred, making a soft cooing noise followed by a snore. They both froze, watching Jonathan, waiting to see if he would awaken. But when he settled down again, Alex turned his attention back to Darren. The man's expression had darkened.

"Careful," he warned. "Don't wake him."

"I know," Alex shot back, annoyed. "I'm sorry. God forbid we get interrupted again."

Darren's frown deepened. "Where is this coming

from?" He pushed his plate away and leaned back in his chair, folding his big arms across his chest as he eyed Alex. "Of course you bring something to this relationship. You're my mate. Without you, I wouldn't have Jonathan."

"Is that all I'm good for then? As your mate? Something from our wolf sides? Something instinctual and almost uncontrollable? And I'm only worthwhile because I gave you a son? I want you to love me for me."

The words made Darren flinch a little. They had never said "I love you" to each other. He didn't realize how much that had bothered him until now. Yes, Darren showed how much he cared in dozens of different ways, sometimes you just had to hear it out loud.

Sometimes you had to have someone say how much they cared.

But Darren didn't seem to understand. "You need to make a choice, Alex. I will give you everything I have, everything I am, but you need to accept it. I can't give up my life here to follow you around the world. We have a child now—"

"Maybe I'm not ready to give up who I was yet." More hot tears flowed down his cheeks. He knew he was way out of line. He didn't even know what he was saying. The words seemed to burst from his lips, full of pain and fear. In his heart, he didn't even completely believe them either.

He had made peace with having a child and leaving the wild, footloose part of his life behind. Hadn't he? It was time to grow up. He had a young life who depended on him now. And he had Darren, who was a good man who seemed to want to care for him and make him happy. Why couldn't that be enough?

Scowling, Darren shook his head at Alex's last words. "It's too late for all of that. That's in the past. We have a child to look after now."

Those were exactly the things Alex had just been thinking, but when Darren said them, they only made him angry and frustrated. He knew he was being a child, but he felt so much pressure and worry. He'd thought those feelings would all go away after the baby was born. He thought he had put things behind him when Darren forgave him for running off and vanishing for months, then showing up on his doorstep again pregnant and nearly due.

God, he was such a bastard. He was unworthy of Darren. The alpha was so much of a better person than Alex was, it just made Alex feel all the more terrible.

"I don't know what I'm doing," he said in a shaking voice, hitching with sobs. "I'm sorry. For everything."

Darren stood and reached for him. Alex knew his

mate meant to comfort him, but he couldn't endure that right now. No matter how much part of him wanted it, he couldn't endure it. He felt like every part of his skin was itching with fear and self-disgust. If a hole had opened up in the middle of the floor, he would've gladly thrown himself into it and maybe even zipped it up behind him.

So Alex moved back out of his reach, refusing the comfort of his mate's embrace. Refusing it even though it was all that he wanted in the world. But Darren wasn't deterred. He still came for Alex. The concern in his eyes made Alex's chest feel as if it were being crushed by rocks. He didn't deserve that concern or any sympathy. God, what was wrong with him?

But before Darren could pull him into his arms, little Jonathan finally stirred awake and began to cry.

Darren immediately turned to him and unbuckled him from his bouncer straps. He took Jonathan into his arms, murmuring to him softly, trying to calm him.

Alex wiped at his eyes, feeling headachy and terrible. He knew he looked like an absolute wreck right now. But what did that matter? He was ruining the one good thing in his life. It was as if he were caught in an avalanche, helpless to stop it.

"Will you…?" Alex started before the words caught in his throat like fishhooks. He forced himself to press on. "Will you watch him for a little while?"

Darren looked at him again. "You know I will, but why? Where are you going?"

"I think I need some air. I just…I just need to get my head on straight. I'm sorry."

More tears blurred his vision. He felt pathetic, needy, and fragile. He didn't know how Darren could stand to look at him.

"I'll watch him," Darren said, his gaze sharp. "I don't have to go into the station today. But this isn't over, Alex. We're going to have a long talk when we get a chance."

Alex's heart fell through the floor. He nodded numbly. Of course. He was going to be called out on the carpet by the alpha. He was going to be put in his place. Or…or Darren was going to kick him out once and for all. Darren was going to take Jonathan for himself and send Alex packing. Any way he cut it, Alex didn't think anything good could come out of the threatened "long talk."

What could he do? He deserved it. It was only too bad he had moved in here and handed back the keys to his dingy rental apartment. Now he didn't have anywhere to go except a hotel. But he would never leave without Jonathan.

If Darren didn't want him in his life…if Alex had

failed as his mate, as his omega, all he had in his life now was Jonathan. The perfect reminder of the perfect man who was looking at Alex right now as if he'd lost his mind. As if he'd melted down into an emotional wreck over breakfast for no logical reason.

Which was exactly what had happened.

His thoughts reeling in his brain, Alex stumbled out of the room. The walls felt like they were closing in on him. It was hard to breathe, and he felt like he might be having a panic attack.

Finally, he pushed his way through the French doors outside onto the back deck. He stood in the dawn sunlight, listening to the birds as he looked up at the blue, almost cloudless sky.

Desperately, he focused on his breathing. He was doing the Lamaze breathing again, trying to find his center, to breathe through the panic that was ripping at him.

He sank down into the chair Darren usually sat in and put his head in his hands. More tears came. He let them come.

CHAPTER TEN

Darren very carefully put Jonathan in the infant carrier. He did it as delicately as if he were defusing a bomb because he didn't want Jonathan to wake up. His little son had fed again and demanded to be entertained or soothed by being carried all over the house.

So he paced through the house, careful to support Jonathan's head as he sang to him softly. He saw Alex outside. His omega was sitting in one of the deck chairs, staring off into the distance as if he had the weight of the world on his shoulders.

Darren's heart went out to him. He wanted nothing more than to charge out there and make everything right again. But first he had to understand where all of this was coming from. Because right now he was totally in the dark. Alex's meltdown had seemed to come out of nowhere.

Was it him? Was Darren just an ass who couldn't pick up when his mate was in pain?

Maybe. He didn't waste a lot of time fretting about emotions. From the moment he'd first seen Alex and his wolf had claimed the omega as their mate, he had only been determined to bring Alex into his life forever. He didn't even like to think of the pain he'd felt when Alex had abandoned him. He had thrown himself into work, taking on extra hours, extra training, all to make sure he didn't waste too much time locked in his head.

He knew he wouldn't be the best person to talk Alex down from any emotional ledge he was on, but he was determined to go out there and listen and try to understand. As an alpha, his tendency was just to charge ahead, to fix things, get things done. Make things right. But right now he didn't even understand the problem.

Darren felt wildly out of touch with his mate right now. For him, these last few months with Alex back in his life—and now with the little miracle of their child in their lives—had felt like heaven. Yeah, a heaven in which they were both sleep deprived, but heaven nonetheless. This was what he had wanted. A family. People to care for. So he was happy. Happier than he'd ever been.

There was only one thing that hadn't been right. He hadn't had the chance to take Alex back into his bed again yet. He hadn't told Alex how much he loved him.

Nightly, he yearned to run his hands across Alex's body. To kiss the man deeply and show his passion for his omega. But the doctor had recommended waiting a month, just to make sure everything healed up. So he had been fighting back that desire. He'd been looking forward to wining and dining his omega wolf as soon as Alex felt up to it. He intended to show the man exactly how much Darren had missed him. He intended to show him so well that he would never forget it in a hundred years.

He suspected that Alex would feel better once they were intimate again. People needed touch, caring. He might be a guy, but he was smart enough to know that. While he was always giving Alex kisses and tender touches, clearly he hadn't been doing enough. Or he hadn't been saying the right things.

That was fine. He was still learning here too. He'd never had an omega wolf in his life before. But he knew in his heart that Alex was the man for him. He simply had to find the best way to show it.

He finished getting Jonathan strapped into the infant carrier and a blanket snuggled around him. Jonathan made an adorable sigh. Darren's heart filled with love as he stared down at the wonderful child he'd made with Alex. It was funny that he'd turned into such a sappy marshmallow as a dad. But he wasn't going to apologize for that. He ran into burning buildings for a living. He could be as softhearted as he wanted.

With the baby squared away and secure, he took the infant carrier with him outside onto the deck where Alex was sitting. It was late morning and a beautiful day out. He could smell fresh-cut grass. He could hear distant traffic, a lawn mower, a couple of dogs barking, someone's stereo playing loud music. But the sounds were so familiar and normal that he found them soothing. This was home. He only needed to help Alex see that this was now home to him as well.

Alex glanced at him but looked away quickly. Darren could see the pain and stress in his face. His eyes were red. He looked exhausted and unhappy. Seeing that made his inner wolf want to rush to the surface. It made him want to do anything and everything he could to make his mate happy. Anything to make him feel safe, secure, and loved.

But he also understood that he couldn't charge in as if he were battering down a door to save some trapped victim. It was clear Alex was on edge right now. He couldn't say he really understood why things had seemed to explode out of nowhere over breakfast, but they had. At least now that they were out in the open, he could work to fix things. He would listen to Alex, let him know that his feelings mattered, and then he would set things right.

Somehow.

He set Jonathan and the carrier down in the shadow cast by the table edge, placing the baby between him and Alex. He wanted to pull Alex into his arms and comfort him that way, but he suspected this was going to be about words instead of actions. He was far better at actions, but it was what it was.

"I want to talk," he said softly to Alex.

"Are you going to tell me what a disappointment I am?" Alex replied, his voice half choked with pain. "Because I already know."

Darren frowned. "You're not a disappointment to me, Alex. You've been exactly the opposite. I don't always understand you, I admit it. But you are far stronger than you give yourself credit for." He made sure Alex was looking him in the eyes so he could see that Darren meant every word he said. "I was disappointed when you left me. But you came back. And that made all the difference in the world."

Alex leaned forward in his chair, resting his arms on the table and looking down at their sleeping child. The tension and worry in his expression eased a little as he looked at Jonathan.

"You saved my life," Alex said. "I owe you everything. And I've repaid you by making a mess of everything over and over again."

"You don't owe me anything, my mate. But I want to win your love. That's what I want to have. I need it. I'm determined to win it any way I can."

A tear slipped from the corner of Alex's eye and ran down his cheek. "I love you, Darren. I… I want you to know that. I've been fighting it, not admitting it aloud because I was afraid of what that meant. What changes that would bring. But right now, I just realized that I can't keep denying it. I love you, Darren. And it's terrifying me."

His mate's words touched his heart. But he wasn't surprised that Alex's feelings were complex. The man spent too much time thinking. He was smarter than Darren, that was easy to see, and that didn't bother him either. He was proud that his mate's mind was so sharp and he was such a creative person, taking wonderful, stunning photos. But he didn't want Alex being terrified of his love for Darren.

"Tell me what you mean," he urged. "Why does

loving me terrify you?"

"Because I feel like I could be happy here with you, making a family. Giving up everything else. I just…maybe I wasn't ready to accept that. My life has always been about traveling to strange places and taking photos. Never being tied down."

"Life changes. Fighting that isn't going to make it less true. And sometimes better things come into your life. I'd like to believe that Jonathan and I are better things."

"I know. You're right. You both are wonderful." He chuckled a little, shaking his head. "Maybe too wonderful. It's making me doubt myself."

"Don't doubt yourself. Know in your heart that I love you. I haven't said that to you, but I've tried to show it every day we've been together." He looked Alex straight in those beautiful eyes. The blue eyes Alex had given to their son. "I love you."

Alex closed his eyes, more tears on his cheeks. "I know. You have shown it to me. I'm the problem."

Darren stood and went to kneel down beside him. He reached out and drew Alex to him. He gave him a kiss, kissing those foolish words away. Showing Alex how much he cherished him.

"You aren't a problem, Alex. Or if you're determined to call yourself one, then you're *my* problem.

A problem that means everything to me."

"How can you be this kind?" Alex said, wonder in his voice. "You're too good for me."

Darren smiled and shook his head. "No, I'm not. But I'm going to hope you remember you said that the first time I forget our anniversary. Or buy you the wrong gift for your birthday. Or a hundred other ways I'll stumble. But you have my word, we're walking this path together. If that's what you want too."

Tears were running down Alex's cheeks. "Yes. Yes, it is what I want. Sitting out here, I finally came to a realization. It isn't black and white. I don't have to give up everything. I can still have my photography, even if I'm not traveling. Besides, living here with you these past few weeks... Now that I sit back and think about it, I feel like I am ready to settle down. I'm ready to settle down and raise our family together. Jonathan...and however many more children we have together."

The thought of more children with Alex made him deliriously happy. "I love you, Alex. I'm sorry I haven't said that enough, but every day from now on, I'm going to make sure you know it deep down in your heart." He grinned. "Besides, having a family doesn't mean we'll never travel again. There are family vacations. Theme parks. National parks. Camping. Fishing trips. And I owe you a long, moonlight run in the woods as wolves. As soon as I find a baby sitter I trust, you're coming with me."

Alex threw himself into Darren's arms, crying and kissing him, clearly as happy right now as Darren was.

Jonathan stirred and made a coo that turned into a snort. Both of them ended the kiss and looked at him, holding their breaths. Neither of them moved, both of them worried the baby was going to wake before he'd had any decent sleep.

Jonathan stretched, his tiny hands bunched, then he smacked his lips. After a sigh, he settled back under the blanket and stayed asleep.

"Whew," Alex said. "The little prince stays asleep. We're safe…for now."

Darren grinned and waggled his eyebrows. A hot surge of lust went through his body. An idea burst into his mind. A way to show his mate how much he needed him.

"Since the little guy's still snoozing, why don't we put him in the bassinet. And then I can show you exactly how much I want you and how very much you mean to me."

The slightest blush appeared on Alex's face. His eyes flashed with heat. "A quickie? How naughty. I'm not sure…"

Darren leaned in and kissed his way up Alex's

neck. "Oh, not a *quickie*. But I promise I'll be gentle. I promise to take my time and give you the best blowjob you've ever had in your life. The doctor can't say no to a blowjob."

Alex giggled. "Do I need a doctor's note?"

"Screw that," Darren said happily. He glanced at the baby. "I'd say we have at least an hour before Jonathan's recharged. Plenty of time for me to rock your world."

"You sound like a man with a plan," Alex replied.

Darren could feel his mate's heart already beating faster in anticipation. Just like his own.

"You have no idea," he said in a voice rough with his growing need. "But I'm going to show you, my little omega. Oh yes, I'm going to show you."

Darren picked up the infant carrier. They walked arm in arm back inside. A family in love. Just what he realized he'd always wanted.

EPILOGUE

Six months later…

Alex carried Jonathan cradled in his arms, bouncing him gently from side to side as he walked through the fire station. It was Darren's birthday, and the station was celebrating this afternoon. Of course, Alex had been invited. The firefighters Darren worked with all seemed to like Alex, and they adored Jonathan.

"I'm gonna say it again," a burly firefighter named Mack said in his deep voice as he handed Alex a soft drink. "That kid is some kinda cute. You two do good work."

Mack was six-four at least, with a shaved head and was built like a brick wall. He was even bigger than Darren, and that was saying a lot. But Mack had also immediately taken Alex under his wing, treating him like a younger brother. He doted on Jonathan, often asking to carry him around and showing him the fire trucks. Alex was glad to know him. Mack had become a good friend…as had most of the men and women who worked at the fire station.

"I'm pretty fond of him," Alex said, smiling down at Jonathan.

Mack laughed. "Fond of him? Both of you worship that boy." His grin grew wide. "Not that I blame you. He's become quite the station mascot. Cuter than a Dalmatian even."

Alex laughed and booped Jonathan's adorable nose. Jonathan blinked at him in surprise and then broke into one of his joyful smiles that lit up his little face.

"I gotta say, being a father has changed Darren," Mack admitted. "He's got that look in his eye. Like he's happy. Content. And you can just glance at him and tell how much he loves you and loves his son. He's a good man. He deserves some happiness."

Alex felt a blush creeping up his neck and heating

his cheeks. "He's made me very happy too. He saved my life. And then he changed my life."

"Let me tell you, you have everybody here at the station pulling for you both. If either of you ever need anything, don't hesitate to come to us. We're gonna be like a second family to the three of you."

Alex's throat was tight with emotion. "Thank you."

Mack wandered toward the station's kitchen, bellowing for the rest of the crew to join him so they could get this party started. There was a cake that needed to be lit on fire.

Darren wandered over from the table full of snacks to where Alex stood holding Jonathan.

The way Darren's eyes lit up when he was looking at Alex warmed his heart every time and never got old. He couldn't believe how much he'd come to love this man, the father of his child. Thank God he had swallowed his pride and made the right choice to return to Darren…and to stay with him. He had been so blessed that Darren was such a good man, protective, strong, but also caring and forgiving. Those weren't always qualities found in an alpha, so he knew he was one of the luckiest people alive to have a man like Darren standing at his side.

"Hey there, handsome," Darren said to him. He

glanced around the room. "Where did everyone go?"

"I think they retreated to the kitchen. I'm going to take a wild guess and say they're lighting the candles on your cake."

Darren grunted. "A bunch of firefighters doing something other than putting out a fire? I'll be lucky if they don't react by instinct and drench my poor cake with a fire hose."

"I think you're probably safe. At least until you're in your eighties and have so many candles you set off the sprinklers."

"I guess you're right. How's the cutest baby in the world?"

"He loves being here. He's looking around at everything, taking in the sights as usual."

"That means he's either going to be a firefighter like his old man, or he's going to be a photographer, capturing the world like you."

"Either one is fine with me. I just want him to grow up happy."

"Me too." Darren leaned in and gave Alex a kiss. "I love you, my perfect mate."

Alex looked up at him, his heart close to bursting with happiness. He was trying not to break down in tears in front of everybody, and Darren was making it hard.

Darren gave him a break by leaning down and

placing the tenderest of kisses on Jonathan's forehead. Jonathan blinked up at him with those big blue eyes. He happily babbled at Darren. Their baby was quite the talker.

Darren's grin as he looked at his son was the most beautiful thing in the world. "And I love you too, my perfect son. I look forward to helping you grow up and learn about the world."

"He's got a great father, so I know he'll make us both proud."

It was obvious that Alex's words meant so much to Darren. But before Darren could say anything more, the fire-fighting crew began pouring into the dining room from the kitchen. Mack was carrying a huge chocolate cake covered with candles. All the firefighters were wearing absurd conical party hats. They were belting out the lyrics to "Happy Birthday to You" off-key and at the top of their lungs.

Alex joined in enthusiastically, while Jonathan blinked and goggled at all the commotion with wide, curious eyes.

After the song ended, Mack set the big chocolate cake down on the long table.

"Hurry up and blow out the candles," Mack said. "Or we're gonna set off the smoke alarms."

Darren raised one eyebrow at Mack while Alex

burst out laughing. With a snort, Darren leaned over and blew out all the candles with one breath.

Mack slapped him on the back. "Guess what they said about the big bad wolf and blowing things down was right after all."

Alex couldn't help joining in with the laughter of the other firefighters.

"You're all a bunch of real comedians," Darren growled. Then a grin broke out on his face. "And hell, I love you guys for it."

He moved back to Alex's side and put an arm around his shoulders again. Mack began to cut the cake and serve out slices onto brightly colored party plates.

"Hey, Mr. Sexy Alpha," Alex whispered to him. "I have a few presents to give you later when we're home." His grin grew naughty. "In private. After Jonathan's asleep…"

Darren looked into his eyes, his gaze heated. His smile was just as naughty. "Well, damn, that sounds like an incredible birthday present." He glanced around quickly. "Is it too early to leave?" He leaned closer to Jonathan. "What about you, little buddy? Feeling tired?"

Jonathan cooed and babbled as if holding up his end of the conversation. They both laughed.

Alex knew he had found his family with Darren and Jonathan, and now with the friends he'd made at the fire station. He had no regrets, no second thoughts. Things happened for a reason, and fate had definitely been looking after him when Darren had saved his life from the fire. Now he'd found true love, had given birth to a child he adored, and he knew he had stumbled his way into happiness. He had no regrets and knew that the future of their little family would be an amazing joy. He couldn't wait.

They settled themselves in with birthday cake, good friends, plenty of laughter, and plenty of love.

~ About the Author ~

Max Rose lives and works in Seattle. She shares her home with a three-legged Dalmatian, two fish, and a husband she thinks is perfect.

Max's books are *The Omega's Heir, To Love an Omega, Reclaiming His Omega,* and *Omega Rescue.*

~ Also by Max Rose ~

Reclaiming His Omega
Max Rose

Can an ex-soldier reclaim his love before their chance at happiness is gone?

Even though he's an omega wolf, Luca Santiago has managed to turn himself into a wildly successful business tycoon, buying struggling hotels and making them profitable again. But things get complicated when a hotel he's trying to buy belongs to the family of alpha wolf Griffin Kent. Griffin won his heart years ago...before leaving him to join the military. He's the one man Luca has never been able to forget. Once again, Luca is helpless to resist Griffin's alpha charms. The wolf shifter effortlessly brings out all the omega traits Luca has hidden away to achieve success. Their passion blazes up from where they'd left off, but loving Griffin brings out all Luca's vulnerabilities again, and after a scorching-hot night together, everything in his life is about to change forever.

After Griffin was wounded and honorably discharged from the military, he returned to his hometown to care for his ailing parents. Griffin is a different man now, struggling with his own demons and under pressure to conform to the burdens of an alpha. His father refuses to sell the family hotels because he wants his son to take over his legacy. Griffin doesn't want anything to do with the business. What he wants is Luca, and this time, he's going to keep him. But when Luca ends up pregnant with Griffin's child, he fears he's not ready to be a father because of his wounds and past mistakes. He's already lost Luca once, and it's looking as if his fears of being a bad father might be driving Luca away again. And this time, he's not sure his heart can take losing the omega he's come to love...

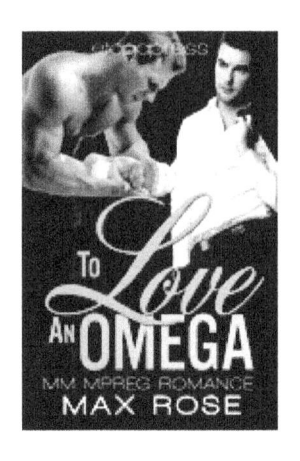

To Love an Omega
Max Rose

He can't stand omega wolves. So why does touching this one set his heart on fire?

Billionaire alpha shifter Jackson Young doesn't like omega wolves. They're weak, submissive, and scheming. He doesn't have time for that kind of man in his life. But when a waiter at one of Jackson's high-powered events spills ice water all over the alpha's tux, he comes face to face with a shifter his wolf immediately claims as mate. Only this "mate" is an omega shifter named Blake Mitchell. As hard as Jackson tries to deny the instant and powerful attraction between them, he soon finds himself pinning the omega to the wall and claiming him with a passionate kiss. That kiss leads to a whole lot of fun...and a whole lot of trouble. After spending a scorching night together, the omega vanishes. Jackson would chalk the whole thing up to a night of no-strings fun, but he struggles to put the shifter out of his mind. Until Blake shows up again much later, very pregnant with Jackson's baby...

After an unforgettably sexy night with the handsome billionaire alpha, Blake returns to his old routine of struggling to make ends meet. He figured that after Jackson got what he wanted from him, the wealthy and powerful wolf would vanish back into his glamorous lifestyle, leaving Blake with only memories. That was fine...until he heads to the doctor for flu symptoms and finds out he's pregnant. Now he has no choice but to track Jackson down again. This time Jackson doesn't seem so eager to see him. He must teach this reluctant alpha that omega wolves can be strong too. Because it isn't only desire that heats their blood and melts their hearts. It's something even deeper.